MY TWO WORLDS

SERGIO CHEJFEC
MY TWO WORLDS

Translated from the Spanish by Margaret B. Carson

Introduction by Enrique Vila-Matas

OPEN LETTER
LITERARY TRANSLATIONS FROM THE UNIVERSITY OF ROCHESTER

First edition, 2011

Library of Congress Cataloging-in-Publication Data: Available.
ISBN-13: 978-1-934824-28-3

Printed on acid-free paper in the United States of America.

Text set in Fournier, a typeface designed by Pierre Simon Fournier (1712–1768),
a French punch-cutter, typefounder, and typographic theoretician.

Design by N. J. Furl

Open Letter is the University of Rochester's nonprofit, literary translation press:
Lattimore Hall 411, Box 270082, Rochester, NY 14627

www.openletterbooks.org

INTRODUCTION

Enrique Vila-Matas
(Translated by Margaret B. Carson)

I begin as I'll end: adrift. And I begin by wondering if novels have no choice but to narrate a story. The answer couldn't be simpler: whether they intend to or not, they always tell a story. Because there's not a single intelligent reader who, given something unique to read, even the most hermetic of novels, would fail to read a story into that impenetrable text. Now then, what happens if the reader is intelligent but the novelist isn't? I suspect that in those cases a great party takes place. I remember Georges Simenon saying that it's absolutely unnecessary for a novelist to be intelligent, quite the opposite: the less intelligent he is, the more possibilities open up to him as a novelist. He was unquestionably right, for I've dealt with great novelists throughout my life and none have seemed very intelligent to me, especially compared to other people I've known, those devoted to other arts, to business, or to the sciences. Of course there are exceptions to this rule. The great Argentine novelist, Sergio Chejfec, is one of them. But if I really think about it, Chejfec is someone intelligent for whom the word *novelist* is a poor fit, because he creates artifacts, narrations, books, *narrated thoughts* rather than novels. *My Two Worlds*, for instance, is above all a book that reminds us that there are novels with stories, but there are also not-so-orthodox novels—Chejfec's are in this camp—though these may also contain stories. The story in *My Two Worlds* isn't easy to summarize because—as is true for all his novels—what's important seems merely an excuse to highlight the dramatic role of the incidental. And so in *My Two Worlds* the narrator's hesitant search makes us ultimately see how the path in the story is etched with disappointment: the walk creates a certain state of mind in the narrator that alternates between fear, confusion, and uncertainty. Insecurity or perplexity can thus be seen in each new sentence, which to us seems the book's new center of meaning (and at last, a valid interpretation of same), though this becomes diluted a few paragraphs later. The author has in part offered an explanation elsewhere, when he talks about his pleasure in seeing how far a sentence can resist, not only in technical terms, but also tonally: sentences are pushed to expand because there's a message, while at the same time they're constrained by a formula, the equation of the sentence. Chejfec is fond of approaching that limit, of making his sentences elastic, not to the point of their incomprehensibility, but yes, of testing that limit to see if it indeed exists. Perhaps that's why he sometimes leaves sentences unfinished, lengthy sentences whose thread is seemingly lost and cannot close. In this way, Chejfec may be showing us that an author not only tells one or several stories, but also struggles or negotiates with the limits imposed by language.

As the writer of this prologue, I face a similar problem in compressing the immense and ever-expanding material of this book. But if I had to summarize it in some way, I'd say we have the story of a writer on the eve of his fiftieth birthday, and that, probably because of that crucial date, he wants to turn into a non-writer.

We'll learn this close to the end, though it's an illusion that gives shape to the story. Not the illusion of writing badly (the impossible dream of the avant-garde), but rather the illusion that the story will disappear into its impossibility, or worse, into its uselessness. In the end, not writing and resigning yourself to an absurd life may be nearly the same as writing and not resigning yourself to anything.

The writer is visiting a city in the south of Brazil, and he decides to walk through its most emblematic park. The long walk, the stroll, takes up almost the entire book. In the park he comes across elements that he discovers are links to his own past, his condition, his identity. The act of describing nature within an enclosed space animates this discreet traveler, who sees in the half-abandoned park (and in the swan boats, the captive birds, the fish and turtles) signs of his own incomplete condition, a cosmic proof that no authenticity is possible.

While the narrator (whose two worlds seem muddled, just as the book at times mixes the essayistic with the narrative) hesitates and has doubts about what he's narrating or, rather, wonders how to do it, Chejfec, in essence, never wonders about it. What's more, he's one of those contemporary writers who have mastered, with utmost skill, both the art of digression and the art of narration. On first reading Chejfec, we recall many admired authors, but at a later moment—a more solid and lasting one—we realize that he resembles no one, and that he has chosen an unusual and quite distinctive path, one which reveals itself slowly because of the demanding and very personal searches the author himself carries out in his narrative.

The pages of this book remind me that from time to time over the course of my life I've come across an intelligent novelist or two. And when I do, I'm often told that it's a shame none of his works have been adapted for film. Surely, this kind of writer—Chejfec appears to be one of them—belongs to a class, still unique today, that must have first come into existence when Marcel Proust showed his contempt for the reductive novel by calling it a *cinematographic parade of things*. I've always thought that kind of a parade—apart from being a simplistic translation of the narrator's interior life—has a pernicious effect; it prevents us from immersing ourselves in a fragment of a story—or in a detail of a fragment of that story—and from devoting ourselves at last to being adrift, joyful at discovering, in the insecure condition of the story of a story, our own world—in reality stripped bare (why fool ourselves) of meaning.

I modestly suggest that Chejfec be included among those novelists who belong to the noblest line of literature in Spanish, more precisely in South America (though Chejfec has the air of being the king of stateless prose), and who for some time now have endeavored to translate their interior life to the genre of *narrated thought*, a genre that, though little-known, has at least escaped with essayistic intelligence from the narrow confines of the great novelists who display an obtuse leaning toward the *cinematographic parade of things*. And in passing I suggest that we think of *My Two Worlds* as a narrative that attempts both to convey an experience of perception and to show, with fictitious indolence, the degree to which a writer of great intelligence can give readers some relief from the everyday and increase their happiness with the sudden realization that they've lucked upon a book that deeply believes that in art, and especially in literature, only those who jump into the unfamiliar matter. Because one doesn't discover new lands unless one has first managed to lose sight of all shores, and for a long time.

I'd prefer not to, but if I had to assign this book to a specific niche within contemporary letters, I'd place it among the liveliest and most decidedly contemporary of novels. I'd locate *My Two Worlds* among the *rarae aves* of recent fiction, among those books still capable of blazing new paths on the perilous trajectory of the modern novel. Its antecedents may be European authors, but also a certain Latin American narrative as well—let's say wide-awake and cerebral—that doesn't quite fit the literary *latinoamericanismo* currently in vogue. Chejfec, in *My Two Worlds*, joins those writers who have no fear of the open sea, and who get along well with readers who have surely, and for some time, been longing to abandon themselves to unstable territories, to get lost in the dramatic realm of the incidental, in that which seems unimportant, "in that which is generally not noted, that which escapes notice, that which has no importance, that which happens when nothing happens, other than the weather, people, cars, and clouds," as Georges Perec would say.

In this sense, or maybe in another—and here I'd like to record my absurd and perhaps entirely useless desire to be neutral about this novel, which I so deeply admire—*My Two Worlds* still seems to me, months after having read it for the first time, the most complete walk I've taken through the ever-incomplete geography of the dramatic realm of the incidental, through the solitary geography of our fissures, through the deep geography of the hollows that are often doors to the unknown, to forgotten places that ignite our imagination and our driftlessness and even our birthday celebrations, which sometimes—on those rare occasions when evening falls in a special way—do not even require that there have been a time lived. Twilight is enough.

MY TWO WORLDS

O nly a few days are left before another birthday, and if I've decided to begin this way it's because two friends, through their books, made me see that these days can be a cause to reflect, to make excuses, or to justify the years lived. The idea occurred to me in Brazil, while I was visiting a city in the south for two days. I couldn't really understand why I'd agreed to go there, not knowing anyone and having almost no idea about the place. It was afternoon, it was hot, and I'd been walking around looking for a park about which I had almost no information, except its somewhat musical name, which by my criterion made it promising, and the fact it was the biggest green space on the map of the city. I thought it impossible for a park that large not to be good. For me parks are good when first of all, they're not impeccable, and when solitude has appropriated them in such a way that solitude itself becomes an emblem, a defining trait for walkers, sporadic at best, who in my opinion should be irrevocably lost or absorbed in thought, and a bit confused, too, as when one walks through a space that's at once alien and familiar. I don't know if I should call them abandoned places; what I mean is relegated areas, where the surroundings are suspended for the moment and one can imagine being in any park, anywhere, even at the antipodes. A place that's cast off, indistinct, or better yet, a place where a person, moved by who knows what kind of distractions, withdraws, turns into a nobody, and ends up being vague.

The day before I had attended a literary conference, and when it was over I walked through the plaza where the local book fair had been set up, in one of the city's historic districts, I assumed, though many relics or landmarks now seemed definitively missing. People were walking slowly, crowding the thoroughfare because of their numbers. I must have been the only solitary walker that day, which luckily no one found strange, because families, groups of friends, or couples went on with their business as I strolled about. Earlier, as I was waiting in an empty room for the conference to begin, I'd read in the newspaper that every year, when the book fair takes place, the regular artisans move their stalls and tables to the adjacent streets. I don't know why that information seemed important to me, and even more, why it stayed etched in my mind. (The following day, a few blocks from the plaza, I discovered the artisans' temporary location, where they'd organized themselves by craft, as if protecting themselves from some danger.) Later, at the end of the panel, I didn't ask any questions; I was, in fact, the first to leave the room, in search of a quick exit to the street. I rode down a glass elevator that looked onto a spacious interior garden, and when I finally left the convention hall, which seemed to have once been a government palace, I had no choice but to join the steady stream of people, like a fugitive trying to blend in.

The layout of that plaza was, as I said, in the old style: a rectangular block with two diagonal and two perpendicular lines that meet at the center, where there's a statue. Despite such a simple design, all the same the moment soon arrived when I felt lost, probably because of the multitudes, to which you'd have to add the dense foliage and the nighttime shadows. I found myself stationed from time to time in front of the same booths; in reality there were only a few offering any titles that aroused my curiosity, which was weak in any case, and only after peering at the tables between the shoulders of an army of onlookers did I realize that I'd already been there, and had of course stopped in front of the same books. But though I sensed a few areas remained to be covered, I wasn't sure which ones I'd already visited. And so I joined the throngs once more and let myself be carried by the flow. I remember that as I walked, the repetition of the strands of incandescent lights made me feel drowsy, just as in some movies. At the rear of the plaza, keeping in mind the orientation of the central statue, and on a short passageway that led to several public buildings, the food stands for the book fair had been set up, and these were also mobbed. Depending on the breeze, the odors from the burners, generally of fried foods or rancid oil, wafted over; at times when I raised my eyes I could see columns of smoke billowing through the strands of lights and the fringed edges of the awnings. Anyhow. I should say that it was this sensation of being hemmed in by the incessant swarm of people that led me to think of the existence of a park I'd like to visit. It would be just compensation, I thought.

One consults the map of the first city that comes to mind and everything seems accessible: one needs only to obey the street plan. But on the afternoon I've been talking about, reality, as is almost always the case, turned out to be different. The retaining walls of the elevated streets, the access roads and overpasses, the ramps for pedestrians or those exclusively for cars—all of them prevented me, at each moment and in different ways, from leaving behind the point I'd chosen downtown for the sole purpose of continuing onward to the park. On the other hand, if I tried to take the long way around, I'd risk getting lost or, even worse, would spend the rest of the day meandering through indistinguishable and unavoidably sad streets; for if the map had proved useless in showing me the shortest way, it was absurd to follow it in taking a longer one.

On one side I had the grounds of a gigantic hospital, like those of years ago, with enormous pavilions and endless gardens. An overpass rose before me, with ramps and streets that didn't seem to go anywhere in particular. And on the other side, an express lane cut the grid of the streets in two. I was, nevertheless, alone in my indecisiveness in this part of the world, because the rest of the people were coming and going, sure of their direction and moving with remarkable ease. I noticed that the more I looked at the map, the less I understood it; what's more, because my eyesight is poor and my glasses aren't strong enough, I must have looked pathetic, since I had to put the map practically against my face in order to see it above my eyeglasses. Every now and then I raised my eyes to the street, hoping to find some point or street sign that would orient me, but I immediately understood that the effort was in vain and I looked down again, spending more valuable time trying to find myself once more on the map. I was like this for a good while. I realized that my sense of direction, which had always been a secret source of pride, and was, in fact, almost the only thing I could brag about, had suddenly abandoned me as well.

And curiously, due perhaps to the never-ending flow of people at my side, no one stopped to offer me any help or to ask if things were all right. I felt invisible, as if I had hidden my face and didn't want to talk to anyone. Then someone went, "*Psst*," toward where

I was standing. It was a street vendor who had to pick up a heavy load and put it in a two-wheeled cart. I thought he was calling me and I looked at him, half-curious and half-hopeful: he probably took pity on me and was waving me over because he didn't want to leave his merchandise unattended. But it turned out he was calling someone else, a young man passing behind me, whose help he wanted to lift the load. So you have to ask for help, I thought . . . I began to imagine the aerial view of that part of the city, probably similar to what was depicted on the map, my silhouette motionless while people and cars continually passed beside me. I don't know why, but that physical image of my solitude or helplessness made me lose patience. Moved by an unjustifiable impulse, I began to rotate the map in order to see it from another angle, and even turned it like a set of handlebars; maybe that would clear things up, I thought. The aerial observer was circling, I supposed, and that's why the map revolved as it did.

On my walk at the book fair the night before, I only began to feel alarmed when I found myself, for the ninth or tenth time, in front of the booth for the local historical society. But what worried me wasn't that on each new turn I felt the same innocence as I had initially, that is, an anxiety to discover an important book, one that perhaps I'd been dreaming of for years without realizing it, and that would allow me entrée to a rather difficult, half-guarded store of knowledge; no, what alarmed me instead was that the repetition I had yielded to no longer exasperated me. Even when I looked upward at the sky, seeking to find something simple and clear to dispel my confusion, I discovered, for the most part, columns of smoke that were rising quickly from the grills, and hardly anything else, nothing that could be found consoling or inspirational. Another booth that had by now become rather familiar to me belonged to the publishers' association, as had one for a bookstore that offered an assortment of popular titles. I wanted to forget the reason I came to the city, and was even tempted by the idea of forgetting my own name and trying to be someone else, someone new.

That touched off a long train of thought not worth summarizing. I'll only say that being someone else meant not so much a new beginning or a new personality, but rather a new world, I mean, that reality and all people in it would lose or cast aside their memory and admit me as a previously unknown member, a recent arrival, or as someone with no ostensible ties to the past. Later on, as I was saying, when the crowds began to tire me, I decided to get a map of the city as soon as I could, to see if it would confirm the existence of that great park, one that was fairly large and that would measure up to my expectations.

By that point I'd almost given up when a fairly obvious idea occurred to me, which under those circumstances seemed providential: it would be best to find my way through the streets by attending to the relative position of places, rather than plotting an exact path or following a sequence of street names. The streets drawn on the map showed routes that were not only impossible, but also unverifiable; on the other hand, the spatial organization of the area could hardly be wrong; it was, at most, approximate, which was, in any case, advantageous, and would save me from needlessly lengthening my journey. By then I was dragging my feet due to fatigue and the sensation of having paced up and down the streets of the city far too long, ever since I'd left the hotel in the early morning, when it was still cool. More than once, after walking along the same block two or three times—unintentionally of course, I'd done so because of chance and disorientation, or frankly, lack of interest—I'd been led again to the same block: and more than once

I thought I'd seen looks of surprise, or maybe simple curiosity, at this outsider who was acting strangely and kept reappearing.

For me, wandering has become one of those addictions that can mean either ruin or salvation. I acquired the habit in childhood, when in the aftermath of an illness I stopped walking. I would sit in the doorway to watch the people and the cars pass by. At that time, using my legs had become a remote and elegant anatomical ability for which I was unprepared, who knows the obscure reasons why, a gift that enabled one to to cover distances. A year later, a new medical report authorized me to stand on my feet again, and to me it seemed that thanks to the word, I'd recovered a physical skill, as if a god had delegated part of his freedom to me. At that early age I could only go to the corner or around the block; but from then on, as successful people say, nothing could stop me. Even before I could understand it with any certainty, in all likelihood I sensed that the main argument in favor of walking was its pace; it was optimal for observation and thought, and furthermore, it was the corporeal experience with the best syntax to accompany one in life. But I'm afraid I can't be sure.

It's true that many things related to walking have changed, some of which I'll refer to in a moment, but the same habit, which I've kept even in times of misfortunes or of ups and downs in general, supports the idea I have of myself as the eternal walker; it's also what's definitively saved me, in truth I don't quite know from what, maybe from the danger of not being myself, something that tempts me more and more, as I said just now, because to walk is to enact the illusion of autonomy and above all the myth of authenticity. The actual habit itself thus helps to sustain that version, because as soon as I arrive in a city, the first decision I make is to go out; I want to become familiar with the surroundings, to permeate it by means of the simplest, handiest, and most convenient act, which is to walk.

As soon as I returned to the hotel, I asked for a map of the city at the reception desk. Given the late hour, and maybe because the staff had gotten in the habit of seeing me come and go all the time, greeting them at every turn and asking questions or making banal remarks, this request took them by surprise. And so I waited a good while, leaning my elbow on the counter. I can't say I remembered ever having had a similar experience, because in truth I didn't remember anything in particular. But I had the clear conviction that I'd been in that kind of situation before. Standing expectantly at hotel counters, the odd world, half-clandestine and half-disjointed, that one steps into while waiting for something at the reception desk. Suddenly a map was placed before me, the sort that folds eight or twelve ways and carries ads for important businesses. My first reaction was to look on the map for the green blotch. It didn't take me long: I saw it whole, almost round, like a barely contained ink spill. I felt relieved to know I'd immerse myself in it the following day. After that I wanted to locate the hotel, something that took more time and that I finally managed to do, thanks to the help of a receptionist. Then I set about planning my walk, which in fact didn't require much preparation; it was only a question of preparing myself mentally.

Though I've enjoyed long walks throughout my life, and continue to do so, to the point of feeling they're an essential part of my true life, a habit without which I couldn't recognize myself, for some time now walking has been losing its meaning, or at least its mystery, and sometimes all that's left is my old enthusiasm, which usually dissipates within the half-hour like a wisp of smoke. I've often thought that the cities themselves are to blame. The visual and economic uniformity, the large chain stores, the transnational fashions and styles that relegate the unique to a secondary level, to a hazy background of faded colors. Finding distinctive features in the streets takes some doing; and even when I recognize them, it's as if the local idiom had fallen silent and the signs of a practical and omnipresent language had been imposed, a well-known language, one that's indistinct, even unnecessary, and lacking manners of its own.

But it's also possible that I myself am to blame; for various reasons, when a certain moment arrives, I can only see what's repeated. I've even begun to notice, to my own mortification, that the breath of adventure—or in any case, intrigue, which has always accompanied me on my endless excursions through the streets of every new or familiar city or locale I visit—gives way more and more often to tedium, short-lived interest, or straightaway to confusion. I walk blocks and blocks, I begin avidly and enthusiastically, that is, I observe everything, not letting the smallest details escape me, but little by little I'm invaded by a sense of lethargy and of surfeit in advance.

It's a feeling of uselessness and imminent boredom. The day seems endless; I think of the hours that stretch ahead as I walk and walk, blocks and blocks, one after the other, the traffic jams, noisy corners, crowds, etc., or the opposite: abandonment, solitude, order, or neglect. And I assume the surprises won't be important, genuine surprises, but will rather be of little importance; on the other hand, I know I was never hunting for surprises, the word "surprise" has always produced rejection, if not downright fear, in me; I understand that my traveler's sensibility, in the private language of thought, admits certain impressions that border on surprise, a state of satisfaction before an object or before a new or unnoticed event, whatever it is, a connection between the past and what's new—and at times a bit exotic—found at that moment in the unfamiliar conglomeration of the blocks in question, etc. The truth is, I've stopped searching for surprises because I believe it's become too difficult for me to find them. And so from my old yearnings I retain a basic mechanism, a kind of physical and at the same time social tic, which is the long walk.

Once I left the reception area I went to an Internet lounge, also located on the main floor, to see if I could check my email. Because it was late, I managed to find a computer that was available. The day before I'd learned that you should go to the Internet lounge during those hours, I mean, late at night, because if you went in the early evening, you'd find people, and likewise, if you went later on, when it was early morning, you'd find insomniacs. I opened my email and was intrigued by an anonymous message, or rather a message from someone who most likely wanted to hide his identity—unsuccessfully, if that was the case. The message had one or two lines, I believe only one, and with an ironic tone, it suggested that I open a link whose content I'd find very interesting or beneficial—I don't remember what it said all that well. I had no reason to doubt it, and so, curious, I followed the instructions. The link opened to a review that had appeared in a newspaper a few days before, about a novel I'd published some months earlier.

The review was rather negative; it said the book was a failure whichever way you looked at it. I pondered the arguments and judged them weak. Then I responded to the sender in two lines, wrote other emails I had to send, read the news from Argentina for an unnecessarily long time, and went up to my room. In all likelihood the anonymous messenger had sought to mortify me, thinking I'd collapse or would give up literature because I'd published

12

failed novels, or novels that aren't novels, I don't remember my exact thoughts. It was strange, because even though I should have been sad that someone wanted to humiliate me and had easily found the tools he believed would be useful in achieving his goal, I was above all comforted by the fact that I'd come across a person evidently worse than me, because that idea would never have occurred to someone better.

For various and complicated reasons, at that time I was fairly dissatisfied with my writing; that hasn't changed, and I can say I've become even more dissatisfied since. While riding the elevator I thought about what had just happened, and a moment later, as I opened the door to my room, using my shoulder because the door seemed stuck, I realized that the anonymous messenger was the product of my own fiction. That my novels, good or bad, had created resentful beings who were condemned to an equivocal servitude. Even I could be one of them. I turned on the television and dimmed the screen so that I could pretend it was a radio. Then I put a book in my small backpack, a notebook for writing, my ID, money, a camera—one of those compact models—made sure I had a pen, and in this way assembled all I'd need for the walk the following day. I still had the map in my hand, which I unfolded on the bed to study carefully.

The television must have been tuned to a local station, that's why it was broadcasting a program about the benefits of soy, its great return on investment, and the care required for its cultivation. Then there was a mini-program about vegetables and their transport. Meanwhile I devoured the map, trying to memorize something that was almost entirely unfamiliar and devoid of meaning for me, for none of the names of the avenues or the arrangements of the streets recalled any hierarchy or visual landscape. Thanks to the map's legend, though, I was able to identify key locations, numbered 1 to 15. But even these critical points were somewhat unforthcoming, because I obviously had no idea what they stood for.

I thought the only thing holding the map on the bed before me was the great green blotch, as I called it. The sovereign park that soaked up the city's presence and radiated energy all along the streets that came to an end there. I studied the map for quite some time, wanting to glean some valuable idea, a kind of preview of the trip, and while deep in concentration I saw a small black 9 printed at the heart of the park, a number no larger than any of the others, the convention surely a great injustice to the city's main sustenance and ultimate justification, and yet the number had a paradoxical effect on me, the reverse of what was intended, for it strengthened my resolve to visit the park the next day, after a foreseeable, or rather, obligatory tour through the center of town and its surroundings, which I had also planned.

In this way, then, my days are dramatizations of a tramp at leisure, of a charmed life spent out in the streets, like the dandy dropping in on a strange world, where he nevertheless fails to find the hoped-for escape. This is perhaps connected to the passage of time, to whose effects we all succumb—though in different ways of course. Every task is cumulative; and if a certain weariness sets in after years of walking up and down the streets, it's logical to think it's caused more by time than by habit. Hour after hour, like a robot, morning and afternoon, like a misfit. I was stupefied by sunsets, at the mercy of a kind of hypnosis by which anything at all made me curious and simultaneously apathetic. A desire to know would animate me just as I sank into aimless drift. Any detail would distract me, though generally for a mere few seconds: the lights of shops, the models of cars, the makes of buses. All but people, because my robot-like walker's inertia kept me from focusing on anyone.

When I come to think about it, my evolution as a contemporary walker—my ideal state being somewhere between curious and skeptical—got sidetracked into my present state as a disappointed and at times infuriated walker, by a process that has dragged on for years. This all started when I began, at the time unawares, searching through urban landscapes for traces of the past. It was a great and irresistible weakness to which I finally succumbed. Conceivably, European cities, and my many walks through them over the years, may have had an influence. These cities, as we know, are famous for venerating their history, or their heritage, and they raise the curtain on a fortunate, bountiful present as an extension of a so-called living past—a past thus revealed as benign. I allowed myself to be carried away by clichés of living ruins and well-preserved artifacts, and the experience must have left me with the kind of sensibility that is conditioned, I suppose, to search wherever I'm walking for traces of forgotten days, even when finding them is rarely worth the effort. Because elsewhere, outside European cities, the traces are of a distinctly different order: they aren't visible as such, or are of a different class, or else there is, quite simply, no apogee to celebrate. Whatever the case, I was defamiliarized, that was the elusive lesson of European cities, which may explain why I go looking for things that can't be found, are basically invisible, or don't exist; and that don't satisfy me when I do find them, since I can't take them seriously. And so my walks have turned into tortuous rituals, driven onward by the indifference that comes from years and years of behaving the same way.

That's why almost everything is leading me to abandon my walks: what I search for, impossible to find, as much as what I discover, practically nothing. And yet an urgent, contradictory force is driving me forward; I cannot renounce walking or stepping out into the street. When I arrive at a given place, my curiosity is triggered at once: it may sound naïve and somewhat vitalistic, but I long to steep myself in the life and customs of the natives, to immerse myself in local habits and idiosyncrasies. A reading to discover, a story to live. But in my mimetic passion there quickly comes the point, which, moreover, arrives sooner and sooner, after I've walked no more than a few blocks: it's the aforementioned weariness, distraction, something I might call "walker's malaise"—a mixture of rage and emptiness, of thirst and rejection. From then on I act like a zombie: I see people as if I weren't seeing them; the same applies to the façades of buildings and the far reaches of streets or avenues. I'm capable of appreciating certain details and recognizing worthy specimens from decades or centuries ago, ambiguous on the whole and fairly deteriorated now, even if well cared for, along with cityscapes and social mores and tics that awaken my curiosity and are unique, etc. But as if I'd ended up consumed by the blind traction of my automaton's stride, intent solely on devouring the pavement until dusk, I instantly forget what I've just seen and taken note of or, rather, I toss it all into a jumbled corner of my memory, where everything piles up at random, with no hierarchy or organization.

So though I'm capable of remembering intersections, scenes, episodes, and generalized small bits of reality, I cannot put them in a sequence, let alone provide any reasonable context, any point of reference. What I saw two blocks earlier is on the same level as anything I saw yesterday, for instance, or a few months ago. Nonetheless I keep walking, propelled, or rather drawn onward, by my sense of ambiguity, by the malaise I spoke of earlier. Perhaps experience, strictly speaking, may be nothing but this; I mean, so much walking has diminished my capacity to feel admiration or surprise: the first block of any city triggers memories and comparisons that undermine the illusion or the confidence one normally places in the totality observed. Things cease to be one of a kind and are revealed to be links in a chain.

An interview program was just starting on the television during which recognized figures from the countryside would talk about their beginnings, about their families, or about the customs of yesteryear, as they put it in the lead-in. It was time to get ready for bed, I thought. I headed to the bathroom and was yet again impressed by its impeccable lighting, like an operating room without shadows. As I came out, a man was speaking whose intonations suggested he was getting on in years. He said that even though he had lived his entire life in the country, he'd never gotten over his fear of the dark, and ever since his childhood had thought of a day's labor—not only his own, but everyone's—as an attempt to avoid or postpone the coming of the night. He was known, the woman interviewing him said in a fawning tone, for his conversational gifts. I couldn't tell, however, whether this was more an invitation for him to keep talking than a compliment. The fearful gentleman was silent while he thought of an answer; at first that's what I supposed, but when several minutes had passed and he still hadn't spoken, I assumed the program had ended abruptly. In the meantime I went in and out of the bathroom again, folded the map, put it in the backpack, got into bed and turned out the light. My last physical act, that I can remember at least, was turning off the television with the remote control, in case the sound came back on.

As I listened to the deep droning silence of the nighttime street, I naturally started thinking about the following day's walk. On one hand, I was excited about getting to know the unknown; but also, as I intimated earlier, I felt I had the right to feel disappointed in advance. I thought of the man on the TV program and his fear, which he had been unable to overcome despite having spent his life in the country, where, as we know, one lives with the deepest, and most threatening darkness, so that he'd been subject time and again to these crises, and must necessarily have had infinite opportunities to conquer his fear. The last thoughts I remember having were about the route I'd be taking in the morning. I had high hopes for a perfect day, perhaps because of that I preferred not to visualize the city in advance; nonetheless something pulled me in the opposite direction too, a growing disappointment, unmistakable and hard to counteract, the result of my single, insistent certainty; namely, that my morale as a walker had been in a bad way for some time.

The reasoning that follows may seem a bit abstract, so I'll expound on it quickly. When I walk, my impression is that a digital sensibility overtakes me, one governed by overlapping windows. I say this not with pride but with annoyance: nothing worse could happen to me, because it affects my intuitive side and feels like a prison sentence. The places or circumstances that have drawn my attention take the form of Internet links, and this isn't only true for the objects themselves, which are generally urban, part of the life of the street or of the city as a whole, shaped precisely and distinguished from their surroundings, but also the associations they call to mind, the recollection of what is observed, which may be related, kindred, or quite distinct, depending on whichever way these links are formed. On a walk an image will lead me into a memory or into several, and these in turn summon other memories or connected thoughts, often by chance, etc., all creating a delirious branching effect that overwhelms me and leaves me exhausted. I'm a victim, that is, of the early days of the Internet, when wandering or surfing the Web was governed less by destiny or by the efficiency of search engines than it is today, and one drifted among things that were similar, irrelevant, or only loosely related. Until one reached the point of exhaustion over the needlessly prolonged Internet journey, with an ensuing loss of motivation to delve (or in my case, walk) any further, and then the moment of distortion would arrive, or of parallel nature, I don't know which, when I would notice that every object had essentially turned into a link, and its own materiality had moved into the background, whose depth was virtual, peripheral and free-floating.

The Internet isn't to blame, that's obvious, but I carry the scars of having passed through that stage of absurd, free-floating links, when surfing the Web was an exercise in fickle relationships. At first it was an apt metaphor for my behavior during these urban strolls, as I sometimes call them, as well as for the associations that come to mind as I stroll, but then the typical slippage or con-tamination took place, and the metaphor ceased being descriptive enough to capture its correlative and itself become a symptom. It's impossible for me to know how different my old-time, pre-Internet perceptions were; they probably were, in diverse ways. Before the Internet, my sense of a city was organized differently: my first im-pressions were stamped with their origins and the specific times, as it were, of their formation; they were bounded by the passage of time and by new experiences. And, in the resulting sedimentation, each memory retained its relative autonomy. But after the Internet, it happened that the same system formatted my sensibility, which ever since has tended to link events in sequences of familiarity, though these sequences may be forced and often ridiculous. Those sequences of familiarity lead to groupings that are more or less volatile, it's true, that nonetheless tend to leave what's unique to each impression on a secondary plane, diluting in part the thickness of the experience.

So that afternoon, when I was just about to give up on getting to the park, the idea of paying attention to the relative location of places, rather than to their literal position on the map, was an especially inspired one, though I can't say if it was due to my reviled free-floating Internet sensibility or to a sudden distracted impulse. I looked the map over one last time and folded it—but didn't put it away, in case I'd be needing it soon—said a mental goodbye to the mechanical uproar that was the street corner, and set out for the park. To get there I proceeded fairly straight on a pavement that was at first hidden, disappearing from time to time under highways or elevated structures. To one side was a medical school, aged buildings of a few, but high-ceilinged stories, clearly paired with the hospital pavilion I mentioned earlier. Further on, the path turned into a broad paved platform where crowds that grew increasingly larger gathered to wait for buses. There were several clusters of passengers, each group evidently waiting for a different bus. In one of the clearings between bus stops I saw the street vendor again, the one with the two-wheeled cart, now asking for help in unloading the merchandise I'd seen him pack up earlier. The man sold women's clothing along with spare electrical parts and batteries. I supposed the weight was in the spare parts and batteries. That's how I began to think about street vendors . . .

That morning, my first thought had been about the man from the countryside. I'm not sure on which river of sleep I'd beheld him during the night, but I remember that just as I was about to wake up and start the day, in a half-awaking that seems like a half-sleep, both states habitual to me, I thought of the man who was afraid of the dark. I couldn't tell if it was daylight yet, but I imagined that if it were still night, and if I were that man, I would be afraid. Then it occurred to me that the word might have been misused in the program. "Afraid" often needs qualification because it can be interpreted in various ways. Maybe he was referring to a kind of uneasy anticipation, as when one says "I'm afraid it will rain," though the word can also refer to something more primal and uncontrollable.

When I opened the curtains I saw the beginning of a splendid spring day. Just below the window and across the street was a building under construction, and above it, since the land rose in that direction, one could see, through a row of leafy, evenly-spaced trees, the dome and the neoclassical spires of what seemed to be the cathedral. I turned on the television to listen as I got dressed. A voice that sounded different to me recited the price of seeds and said grains would be coming up next. I remembered how at the book fair the previous evening, each time I passed the booth for the local historical society I saw titles dealing with agrarian subjects, which of course reminded me of Argentinean culture in its rural, pampean, primary-school dimension, I'm not sure what to call it. I wanted to have a coffee quick and head out to the street, so I finished putting my things in order and went into the bathroom.

Once I was in the downtown of another city and saw a street vendor being robbed. I suppose he had just begun to set up or was about to leave; in any event, he was leaning over some cardboard boxes with his back to the merchandise. A passerby noticed he wasn't paying attention, moved closer to the table, and carried off a bag of scarves or pashminas, whatever they're called. That caused me to reflect that street vendors are at their most vulnerable, or simply at their weakest, when they're setting up their goods or stowing them away. The street was busy, with people on all sides; and yet I was the only one who noticed what had happened. Even the victim himself, when he turned around, kept arranging his things as if nothing was wrong. A moment later he sensed that something strange was going on because his display had changed, things were missing, though he probably wasn't sure, either. This tempted me to tell him he'd just been robbed, but I held off because I couldn't explain why I'd taken so long to say something to him. So I looked behind me, as I always do, and above the mass of pedestrians I saw, a block away, the person who had taken the bag, a rather tall man who every so often glanced sideways as he went down the street, in case there might be any danger in pursuit.

As I've seen on other occasions, some vendors never stop unpacking and setting up their stand for the entire workday. They're the ones harassed by the police. They lay their merchandise on the ground or on a flimsy tarp, or hold a lightweight board in their hands, and are more on the lookout for a warning signal than for the approach of the unlikely customer. The police, in their zeal, can be quite meticulous. Several days before the one I've been recounting here, as I stood on a downtown corner in another Brazilian city, I watched three or four policemen chase off a vendor, who, in his haste, left behind a wooden horse he'd clearly been using to support the board that held his merchandise. It was a solid horse, which resisted the kicks one policeman was giving it with all his might. Another policeman intervened and propped it diagonally against a tree trunk, so as to split the wood more easily. A strategy of no use either. Finally, as I was walking away, I saw two policemen jumping up and down on the horse, trying to break it up while the other officers looked on, engrossed by the operation and no doubt intrigued by the object's resistance. I could go on with my reminiscences of street vendors . . .

For instance, while living for a time in a provincial city I encountered, on a daily basis, a woman who sold embroidered tablecloths and napkins. She didn't use a table, chair, or any other support, but stood on her perennial corner for hours, from midday until dusk, holding her goods in her arms and draped over her shoulders. She stepped forward timidly when she thought that a passerby, usually another woman, might be interested in her merchandise. Otherwise, she preferred to stand still, from time to time moving in circles to stretch her legs, I suppose. Seeing her walking like that I was reminded of those picketers in the United States, usually few in number, who circle round and round in the same spot, as if their protest were a kind of punishment.

Now and then, this woman was joined by another woman, who sold flowers from a bouquet, one at a time perhaps, since no other bouquet was visible. She stood against the wall, as if sinking into it, and looked as if she were waiting for someone who wouldn't show up. The two of them made me wonder if some intermediate category existed to describe them, something between a street vendor and itinerant peddler. I remember that as I passed them I tended to think of tango songs, the stories and scenes described in their soap-operaish lyrics, perhaps a line at most, or I would think of movies recounting the lives of long-suffering people, set in another century or another era. People punished by poverty, victims of society and their neighbors, with no means of self-defense and survival other than their dignity. Pathetic, humiliating, and tragic stories. These belonged to a long era that I had, I suspected, for the most part missed, though it was familiar to me, depending on how one defines "familiar"; anyhow, it was a cultural era that I'd experienced, though only at its tail end—which might explain the flurry of songs and movies with such motifs—and in such a way that it had no deep or direct influence on me. And why hadn't it touched me more? Because I'd been privileged, I thought, that's why. The waves of evil and the world's tragedies, multiplied by the number of people who had suffered them and suffered them still, had ebbed, along with their sentimental effects, before they reached me. It was as if at that moment an inner voice had declared: "This guy"—me—"is spared." The misfortunes of the world didn't touch me . . .

If I compared myself with those two women, I would be relieved and somehow consoled, and my sense of well-being confirmed, though in truth my well-being was quite modest, and not all that far-removed from the state of both women. And even though I'd experienced my own share of ups and downs, and suffered mishaps, failures and humiliations, this didn't change the nature of my situation. Whenever I contemplated lives like those two women's, I was mesmerized by I don't know what kinds of memories and fears, and I would compare myself with the most wretched, the most unfortunate, the dregs of urban humanity. From one angle, these comparisons were an obvious comfort; from another, they were hugely disturbing. At my age, to worry about stupidities conceived at the margins of history and of each life's coordinates, mine in this case, exposed the same obscene abundance to which I was accustomed and that I'd naturalized to the point of considering it obvious and guaranteed. Nonetheless, it also showed the quicksand on which everything rested.

No other street vendor made a greater impression on me than those two women, about whom I knew nothing, neither their situation nor their nationality, let alone their names, or whether they had families, husbands, or children, though I assumed they did, and that they, too, were going through hard times. I could imagine these women getting dinner for their families with the little they brought home, the ensuing meals that were shared in a silence fraught with repressed anger and massed reproaches. Or the opposite: the carefree, optimistic joy of scarcity, the good fortune of living in the moment. It's very likely that on the days before or after I saw the women, and more than once during my stay in that city, since I was there for a long time, I crossed paths with people who were still worse off, true outcasts and exiles from human society, with no family and, most likely, no identity, who faced tremendous physical challenges, etc.; nevertheless, not even the most wretched individual elicited a fraction of the anguished compassion that the floating presence of these two ladies inspired in me as they tried to hide the fact that they were selling fairly superfluous merchandise.

No need for anyone to think much about why. The women affected me deeply because unlike other street people or enterprising sidewalk vendors, they were, in their shyness and solicitude, and even in their modesty, an image of myself; that is, I would have behaved the same way if I had shared their fate. I thought: They're not good at this, and I wouldn't be either; they're there because they have no choice, circumstances forced them into it, as they might have forced me as well; they feel ashamed, probably unjustifiably so, but uncontrollably—just as I would have.

One afternoon I entered a small café, no bigger than four tables, near the corner where the women stood. It was going to rain at any moment and I told myself it would be best to wait it out while having a coffee. I took a seat in the back, my preferred spot for looking at everything that interests me, although, given the dimensions of the café, in this case the perspective was limited. Only after I'd been sitting there for a good while, thinking of almost nothing, did I glimpse the flower-seller hunched over the counter. At that moment she was taking small bites of something she held in her hands; I couldn't see what it was because she didn't once pause or lower the food from her mouth. Most likely it was a sandwich, or plain bread, the typical stale piece given to beggars. I understood that way of eating as another sign or example of her repressed state, or perhaps more exactly, in-hibition, because if there was anything revealed by those minimal gestures, it was her guilt or shame. Anyhow. Afterward it began to pour outside. The woman had by now finished the sandwich and for the rest of the time she sat with her head turned toward the street, avoiding my gaze as if she didn't want to be observed.

I now proceeded according to a territorial intuition, if you can call it that, and at the end of a new and lengthy stretch of pavement, during which I came across several bus stops that were mobbed, inevitably, with people, I finally made out the park, that large green mass inside the yellow city of the map. As I walked toward it on a heavily trafficked avenue, so wide that when I crossed at a light I hardly had time to reach the pedestrian island, the green tree tops in the distance seemed exaggeratedly compact, like gigantic broccoli, with the flattened shade of the park beneath its branches, almost cavernous or jungle-like; as I went along it occurred to me that the contrast between the voluminous green and the city encir-cling it was an analogy, clearly deliberate, for the physical condition of the country as a whole, and even, you could say, for its satellite image: the Amazonian jungle and its emerald-green life, extensive and complex, in contrast to the materiality of the Brazil that was economic or urban or constructed, I don't know what to call it.

I took advantage of a path that opened off the avenue to enter the park, not far from the traffic light where I had crossed. Trees with low canopies stood on either side of the path and overarched its entire length, which at first, until my eyes adjusted, made me feel I'd unexpectedly come upon a secluded and astonishingly dense grotto. As soon as I'd stepped inside the park, I realized I had found what I referred to earlier, my secret dream: the park was too large not to have that air of abandonment which so appeals to me. The shadowy, and above all, overgrown edges of the path exuded that unique mixture of neglect, dirtiness, and danger which puts one on the alert; and the truth is, I didn't need to go very far before I'd verified my impression, since when I looked down I saw that the faded gravel had scattered and turned nearly to dust, suggesting that the path was sporadically used and infrequently maintained. Even the shapes of those pebbles, all similarly rounded, like seeds from an almost barren tree, made me realize I was walking on a surface typical of underused parks, where dust, earth and time— the sand of cities—accumulate with nobody's help.

As I walked on along the path, the noise of the avenue began to subside, in great part owing to a curve that as a dramatic entrance seemed, at first sight, to have been a success: visitors had to change course immediately, which not only helped them put the city noise quickly behind them, but also signaled that they could lay down whatever burdens they'd presumably carried in from the street. For the attentive observer, the biggest challenge was locating the precise boundary between path and forest, or terrain, I don't know what it's called, the park preserve. Because anyone who looked closely, as I did, would see a strip of diffuse matter, insistent even in its ambiguity, containing elements from both sides and impossible to classify. This can probably be said of all paths of any kind, but at that moment I interpreted it as a visitor's second lesson, possibly harder to assimilate but perhaps more lasting in its effect; though that required greater powers of deliberation than I could imagine at that moment.

When I came out of the bathroom that morning to finish dressing and set off at long last, I heard a familiar voice on the television. It was the man who was afraid, talking about other subjects; now it was the care and feeding of animals. In the country, he was saying, livestock should be raised with care, and as for wild animals they should be regarded with respect. I guessed it was a children's program, though why, if that were the case, was the man's fear of the dark considered so remarkable? The interviewer, a man now, was asking about further differences between domesticated and wild animals. The answer surprised me: Wild animals never seem tired, because when that happens they hide themselves, whereas domesticated animals always move languidly, and seem tired even when they're not. I was expecting a more classical distinction, and then, I don't know why, I felt I had to do a recap . . . I was in my hotel room, sitting on an unmade bed, in the south of Brazil, I had visited a book fair the day before after coming out of a conference, then afterward read a so-called anonymous message and before I went to sleep had listened to the same person I was hearing now, except talking about something else.

I told myself that perhaps it would be a good thing to keep on listening, and as I listened more closely I detected a certain spiritual hedonism in the voice of the man who was afraid, which made me wonder whether he might be some kind of guru or preacher, maybe a rural mystic given to changeable opinions. Very likely, I thought, he was a guest at the book fair. I was intrigued by the form of his eloquence, his nonchalant air that made no distinction between what was central and what was secondary in what he was talking about, a trait that perhaps reflected a certain insecurity or else rote memorization. In the end a rather unexpected and above all revealing thought occurred to me: I had only to use the remote control to see his face, but I didn't because for a moment I dreaded that I would see my own image on the screen. Perhaps the anonymous messenger was about to reap his reward, because the impact the man who was afraid would have on me would be the most resounding success of his campaign. I imagined myself speaking like that from that moment on, and, still worse, writing like that, too, forever following the most haphazard thoughts in a tortuous way. But I understandably wanted to stop thinking like this, so I turned off the television, gathered my things, and went out in search of my coffee.

Generally, when I walk I look down. The ground is one of the most revealing indicators of the present condition; it is more eloquent in its damages, its deterioration, its unevennesses, and irregularities of all sorts. I'm referring to urban as well as rural ground, difficult or congenial. And I'm specifically referring to the ground of paths, to ground altered by humans in general, because ground in the abstract, the ground of the world, speaks different, near-incomprehensible languages. Walking is, in part, a kind of superficial archaeology, which I find greatly instructive and somehow moving, because it considers evidence that's humble, irrelevant, even random—the exact opposite of a scientific investigation. It's evidence that, because of its unimportance and its secondary nature, restores a way of inhabiting time: one is an eyewitness to the anonymous, to what history can't classify, and simultaneously witness to what will survive with some difficulty. And for that reason, when I walk on paths I've been inclined to leave behind faint, minimal marks—the proverbial initials or the name drawn in the dirt with a stick, ephemera that vanish quickly from the ground or from walls, like sodden footsteps on a rainy day or shoe prints. Not because I believe someone will decipher them in my wake, but because the action implies an innate impulse, one can only hope to leave fleeting traces. Similarly, I regard the random things that make up the path as simple and moving: the blending of varied materials, the wear and tear of age, the former uses, etc., that are at times revealed and which transport me to the lethargic scale of banal discoveries, even predictable at times, yet transcendent because they evoke the secondariness I just mentioned. In fact, one of my greatest weaknesses are those paths that are sometimes traced onto sidewalks and public stairways, the result of countless steps of people in a given place, like an invisible mechanism.

The shaded path I was following would soon yield me its first surprise, something like a second aid in forgetting all about the city I'd left behind me a few meters back. The path opened onto a fairly large clearing, roughly fifty meters wide, where there was a labyrinth (the name I prefer to give it) of greenery, or a circular garden, formed by dwarf hedges, barely knee-high, that delineated narrow, sinuous paths and the odd allée, itself interspersed with flowering shrubs, probably rose bushes, proportionally spaced. Across from me, on the path that encircled the garden, were two bougainvilleas near-bursting with vivid purple blooms. I remember it because their brilliant color stood out from the light green of the stand of trees and the dark green of the hedges. The garden also contained several main paths with a few granite benches, very low to the ground, where visitors could presumably rest.

When I emerged from the darkened path, the light was so dazzling I had to squint. At first the garden seemed deserted, and the silence, because it related to an open space, suggested an absence, I could say an emptiness, or rather, time entirely undefined. Gradually the idea took hold of me to avoid encountering anyone, a thought that occurs to me more and more frequently of late. I stood still and looked at the garden; I wanted to familiarize myself with it, to enjoy the perspective, I don't know, to enjoy the experience of one of those suspended moments associated with picturesque landscapes, apparently definitive in their composition, or at least conclusive because of the idea of harmony, no matter natural or artificial, that they meant to convey; so I found myself standing attentive and motionless to one side of the labyrinth, when all of a sudden something happened: a few meters away from me a shadow materialized that I hadn't noticed until that moment. Some thing or being was hiding in one of the central walks; I couldn't see it clearly at all because of the glaring light, but also because the bench where "that something" was installed was so close to the ground that even the dwarf hedges blocked my view. At first I thought it was a parcel, or more precisely a bundle of forgotten clothes, or some strange animal, asleep and dressed in human clothes, or all three at once. But the next instant I saw it move again; the shape suddenly stood up and walked off, as if unaware of my presence. I couldn't, however, be sure.

I imagined it might be a student from the nearby university, since the figure's backpack, which was pretty large, seemed to hold books or notebooks. What I had taken to be a flattened bundle may well have been the figure's back, or his prone body: he had very likely been reading, or sleeping, or maybe he was weeping or cursing, there was no way to know, or was feeling crushed, or simply bitter and hopeless.

It's happened to me in different circumstances: I believe I'm alone, in a deserted place and completely isolated and on my own, when an unexpected motion or careless glance will suddenly make me realize, alarmed, that somebody else is present. I don't care for those visitors or witnesses who have arrived beforehand and are

31

slow to make themselves known. Even if they did come first, and thus have certain prerogatives—which ones, I don't know—I eye them warily, as if they'd burst in upon my peace, interlopers or nuisances spoiling my contemplation or enjoyment, if indeed that exists. Conversely, I keep an open mind toward those who arrive after I have, because they make me feel like an explorer who for a brief moment is accompanied before taking up his path once more.

As I watched the student receding into the distance, I felt somewhat perplexed, or almost frustrated. At first I thought it was due to the manner in which I'd encountered him, to its abruptness, or to my surprise, etc., but then, when he disappeared from sight, my discomfiture turned to befuddlement and I began to doubt his very existence. The memory was fresh: first, the indiscernible shape, the dark clothes, the quick stretch of the limbs, before he presumably returned to classes or went home, surely necessary after such a long rest; I had seen all of that, and nonetheless couldn't verify that it had happened. Because the truth is that, just as I've described, on several occasions I've been present at a similar scene, as an "intruder-host," and it's also happened that at other times I've had the experience of sighting ghosts, amphibious or spectral beings— erratic figures, fleeting or lazy, that arrive, are present or pass by, but always ignore me.

These unreliable and of course unpredictable beings I see from time to time follow a regime that I'd describe as floating. They seem available, open to establishing contact, or at least within one's reach, and capable of sensing our approach, but they float or are soft: when we draw near they move away, pushed by the ripples of air our movements create. They're unstable, not so much in their fleetingness as in their haphazardness; seemingly dominated by forces beyond them, one moment they're close, then far away the next, or suddenly gone. I don't know whether they sink or rise, or whether they hover in place before passing through the next wall or acquiring another shape.

As I say, I can't rule out the possibility that my impressions have been caused by weariness, built up over a long day of walking, but the ghosts have had a lasting, if indeed ephemeral, presence in what I more or less conventionally call my life, a presence that continues to this day and will no doubt extend into the future. Most often, I don't need to see them to know they're around, or at least to bear them in mind and notice their throbbing presence. They appear according to their own mysterious schedule and settle in an indefinite place for varying lengths of time. From my point of view, they're witnesses, but from theirs, I imagine, they're the protagonists. Still, I've never seen them depart from their script of passivity, nor am I certain that they're contemplative. To my mind, they're hollow, vacated characters, like wandering souls searching for a time or substance that can contain them. Apart from this, I lack Gothic proclivities: the ghosts who accompany me from time to time have never proposed anything, no one is channeling through them, and their productivity is zero. These same deficiencies predispose them to anything at all, as if they were always ready for any sublimation. In an ever-narrowing world with fewer and fewer embellishments, they too have thinned out, I believe.

Today they are fog and shadow, or the blurry speck of a furtive presence. Despite their apparent uselessness, the ghosts have served to rekindle my desire to wander. All too frequently, as I've said, I feel walking lacks a purpose, when I'm confused by my surroundings I forget the reason for my walk, but the ghosts rescue me, they wake me up because in their uncertain presence I'm transported elsewhere to a place, I'm not sure what to call it, where parallel events occur. Then the walk turns into an invented affair, which can unfold as a drama or comedy and, in that way, offer some lesson, though probably a diffuse one. This doesn't always happen, only on the infrequent occasions that my thoughts begin to stray, and it lets me keep walking as I had planned.

I then thought about the apparition of the student. That had no hidden meaning for me, and as I said, the only feeling or aftertaste was one of irritation, first because of my uncertainty about its true condition and, second, because it had taken me by surprise. I took a few steps toward the heart of the circular garden; I felt like a lumbering giant, out-of-scale with the place. Though I needed only to lift my leg slightly to step over the hedges and shorten the way, I obediently kept to the paths. On the central allée I found the bench, looking more like a gravestone, where the ghost had been and, around it, traces of recent use that delighted my archaeological eye, at least that's what I thought, though I couldn't be sure. The earth disturbed near the bench, for instance, which suggested that the character had scuffed his feet against the ground while seated. I could easily imagine a ghost doing the same, I myself would have done so: a typical act in solitude, when one is sleeping in a park, or is feeling desperate, or when one hopes to attract the attention of someone in the future. And when this student had achieved that, he could leave; his intention was to give me something to think about. It was odd that I hadn't seen him at first; and that now, when he was no longer there, I focused on these traces as if impelled to recreate his presence. It's something a walker always does, though nothing seems certain. This afternoon I was facing no solemn or imposing landscape, nor was its physical layout transcendent; it was, as I said, a deserted garden, circular in shape, that if not for the bougainvilleas would have presented a decidedly dejected appearance.

34

I now realize that almost everything in this city has looked that way to me because of the pale, half-dejected light. Perhaps it's the latitude, so far south. Several scenes and vistas reminded me of other cities located on southern rivers, I don't know the best word for them. One can describe cities in many ways, but in their case I'd use the word "quiet." Cities in repose, quiet cities where the waits are always long and must be endured by all . . .

After leaving the labyrinth, or the flower garden, whatever it was, I went on further into the park. I headed down a straight path into which smaller paths converged every now and then. At some of these intersections there were small buildings, painted antique yellow and rounded in shape, resembling guardhouses or observation points, or indeed tiny astronomical observatories, each with its dome, its arched doorway and its narrow window that let in a small amount of light, designed in what appeared to be the Rationalist style. Their harmony of form caught my attention, as did the special care that was devoted, no doubt in the past, to such ancillary structures in what now seem out-of-the-way places.

On the opaque, corroded wall of one of these structures I saw a mark or legend that I couldn't understand, in an unknown alphabet, neither sophisticated nor rudimentary. For a time I tried to decipher it, a single character at least, and as I did so I kept stepping backward and forward, or approaching the wall from different angles. Before giving up, I took a photo, which I've kept, that unintentionally included part of the window, which now, by a trick of photography, resembles an arrow pointing to the incomprehensible script. Someday, I thought, a future walker will be able to understand what the walker from the past left here; he or she will be able to know if it was a warning, an instruction or a private message. And the same applies to the photo I have before me, I think now. Though who can tell what the future holds for a photo that hides beneath its file name on the computer screen—minimized as they say—for the most part dormant. When I click on it, the image unfurls like an apparition, at once sudden and controlled, and seemingly always available, as is everything in my private archive. Nonetheless, its future is known, much as one might wish to ignore it: the photo will live briefly in somebody's memory, and then become dormant once again—that is, in no one's active memory—and after that it will hibernate in some electronic corner of the world for a long time before disappearing for good. In the other photo, which I took so as to capture the entire building from the ground up, you can make out, on the eave or cornice above the doorframe, several patches of peeling paint.

After taking the photo and resuming my walk, I soon came to a shady crossing where several paths converged. It seemed sunk in one of those silences that are supposedly constant yet are called deep, a silence that at first seems perpetual but in fact is made up of many noises. There, under the shade of several giant trees, you could forget the city, or if it came to mind, believe you were outside it, many kilometers away. I took a few tentative steps, fairly surprised by the peace and calm of the place, as if it had been especially designed to confuse, a possible trap, and discovered that the shadows were due not only to the stand of trees and the dense foliage, but also to enormous aviaries, that is, high-ceilinged cages with black-painted bars, which stood in groups of three or four on a wide stretch of the land. The section of the aviary was surrounded by a wire fence. You could see the cages through this fence, at any rate those of them that faced outward, and the birds in captivity were visible within, along with smaller birds who had entered to eat.

I followed the fence until I found the gate, also made of wire and closed with a padlock, where there was a sign saying that on Mondays—that day—it was closed. I looked inside the cages closest to me, which held birds of prey. The cages held two or three birds, each bird well-separated from the others, as if they belonged to different or feuding families, though none were easy to distinguish, perhaps because of the dim light, or their statue-like immobility, which concealed them in the gloom. My eyes picked them out in the shadows, and the first thing I saw were their immense beaks, often in vivid colors and outlandishly shaped, disproportionately large in relation to their heads, though fairly insignificant compared with their bodies, as is generally the case with birds.

These large birds appeared to be asleep or to keep a vigil composed of stoicism and waiting, while they tolerated the visits of individuals lower down the scale who stole in between the bars to eat the food. I was surprised to see a number of sparrows bobbing themselves eagerly over low mounds of ground meat, or meat that had been chopped mechanically into small pieces and spread on long trays. The large birds looked on, unperturbed, at least that was what I supposed, because it was impossible to verify that they were looking at anything in particular. And something else that surprised me was the fact that the sparrows, despite their small build, which would have allowed them to avoid obstacles and fly comfortably between the bars into the cages, crept in slowly, as if they wanted to remain unnoticed, and so make their giant relatives think they belonged to a different species.

The labels with the names of the birds were green with small white letters. The scientific names had a certain morphological resonance for me, but I found the popular names more picturesque, for these were indigenous, or half-adapted, names, which in my imagination recalled divinities or characters from the native mythology, lore that still resonated for the inhabitants of the deep jungles and the great savannas, or had once done so. The only vivid colors to be seen in the darkness were, as I said, the beaks of the raptors and the piles of meat, the former red as well, for the most part, so that one's gaze fell involuntarily and every so often on those two points.

I was busy verifying these impressions when I saw an older, almost elderly woman who was approaching me from one side, presumably to tell me something. Her hair was graying and she wore loose-fitting clothes, as if she lived near the park and had only to put on a presentable bathrobe to visit. Nonetheless, she carried an elegant pocketbook and another object I can't identify now, which at the time seemed like a flimsy parcel, made from used paper or plastic bags. When she reached me, she asked why the aviary was closed, she had made a special trip from home and now discovered that she couldn't get in. I couldn't think of an answer. My first reaction was to conceal the hand holding the map, because I was afraid she would realize I was a visitor and rule me out as a possible helper.

There was the sign in front of us showing the visiting hours and the day the aviary was closed, but since I was a stranger in town it occurred to me that the sign could be old or that there it was customary to ignore it, and that the neighborhood woman was asking me about something else, a more fundamental matter, or for some news that wasn't immediately obvious. I was about to tell her I didn't know, but instead pointed to the sign indicating the aviary was closed, or maybe told her at the same time that I didn't know; in truth, I don't remember all that well. Whatever the case, for a brief moment the two of us stood waiting for something to happen.

Then, as it tends to occur, there was a screech of a bird from above, half-mixed with the revving of a distant motor. I began to think: the coincidence was too great for the sign to be incorrect; so despite its being my first time in the park and at this aviary, which I would be unable to visit any time soon, or maybe ever, since I planned to leave the city the following day, I once more relayed the first and probably last piece of information I'd acquired on this subject, and I told her that the place was closed on Mondays. By way of argument I pointed to the sign once more.

As has happened to me on other occasions, and continues happening to this day, the woman thought it reasonable to ignore me. Something about the way I speak must cause this; it's probable that my lack of conviction in saying even the most obvious things, or the things I most believe in, works against me at times. Most likely, I thought, the parcel she's carrying has food for the birds who spend their entire lives caged and eating nothing but the same old ground meat. She told me she knew it was closed on Mondays. To that I could only insist that today was a Monday. It was a fact I could be sure of despite being a stranger in town, because obviously it was Monday in all of Brazil and the rest of the continent. She stood there thinking, and I noticed how for a fraction of a second she was mentally transported to another place, or another time; she seemed to be taking inventory, and wiping the slate clean. She finally sighed, acknowledging her error, and told me she had made a mistake and would have to go home and come back the following day.

I was more or less convinced that she lived nearby, and from the way she described the operation (have to go home, come back the following day, etc.), it was clear that she treated these visits, which were no doubt frequent, or in any case regular, as events that required preparation and, above all, represented a high point in her daily routine: a duty, a regular habit. That suspicion, if that's the right word, allowed me to glimpse the net weight of a normal life, of any life, to allude to it in a perhaps condescending manner. The skein of a person's own acts, whether unnoticed, essential or absurd, which range from the unconfessable to the naïve, from the irrational to the repeated, each with its dose of fear and dignity. I imagined this lady walking through the fairly empty streets of the surrounding area; two blocks before arriving home, she would think about the best moment to take her keys from her pocketbook and clutch them in her fist until she reached the front door. Most likely, I thought, the spot is predetermined: when she passes a certain tree, or crosses at a corner, she looks for her keys, and when she's found them she removes her hand from her pocketbook. The operation is unconscious, however, just like the "thought" she has before she decides to take out the keys. A thought that is definite and vague at the same time.

I don't know if any of the birds could have noticed our brief conversation; in any case I'm certain no one saw us, because this area seemed separated from human time, as did nearly the entire park for that matter. On one afternoon quite some time ago, at the end of one of my long days of mechanical strolling, during a period of isolation in which I did nothing but read and walk, as two different and yet sadly related activities—I'd forgotten about work and about the world, which didn't bother me a bit, though I'd suffer the consequences soon enough—one afternoon I collapsed in exhaustion at the end of one of my long walks, and for something to do I opened the first book that came to hand. Halfway down the page there was a description of a bird's gaze; and I don't know if it was due to exhaustion or surprise, to my situation in general or the particular eloquence of the story, but the fact is that I was immediately overwhelmed by suggestibility and fear. The impact was such that I had to stay in for several days, probably frightened I'd run across some bird, even at a distance. Since then I've been unable to look a bird in the eye without reliving, more than my fear, the terrifying memory of that moment. Because sometimes the memory of what one has read tempers the actual experience, and the experience itself becomes, more than something physical, the realization of the reading . . .

The bird should remain at rest and the observer, whoever it is, perhaps myself, should stand in front of the creature, at some distance or closer-up, but facing it straight on. This exercise is impractical with fidgety birds, in general the smaller ones. It is the larger birds, much higher up the scale, and a few medium-sized birds, or those slightly removed from the aerial world, roosters for example, that make a greater impression. When you look at them you receive a terrible shock, because it's hard to avert your eyes. It's much more complicated than looking at fire, of course, because while the flames elicit an innocent fascination, which lets you have thoughts that are distant in time and space, the gaze of a bird induces the most anguished stupor in the observer, such that the bird's violent origin can be seen; that is, both poverty and delirium at the same time. Afterward, in my experience, and in that of others who have mentioned theirs, it's advisable and with effort, possible to turn your eyes from the creature's transparent gaze, but it's impossible not to turn them back to it again. You may think you've broken free, but unawares you are once more unavoidably drawn to the same icy, never-ending stare.

I remained observing the aviary a little while longer. A few of the large birds had changed their places, and now a pale beam of sun lit up their beaks from above. And the spatial counterpoint their beaks created with the meat almost on the floor had intensified, so much so that for a moment I imagined that my eyes were the vertex of a rather large angle: one line represented my downward gaze at the birds' red meat, while the other shot upward, where the beaks could be seen.

The shady path I had come along continued toward the park's interior. I caught sight of a bright point toward the end of the path—the afternoon light, as it turned out. I headed in that direction, since I intended to keep strolling through the park and the idea of a slight change in scenery appealed to me. Before I left the canopy of trees that surrounded the aviary, I looked back several times, a habit of mine, and was struck by the color of the ground in the aviary and its environs. It seemed like another surface, not dirty but dirtied, though no stains or traces of garbage were visible. It had a different shade of color, most likely owing to the birds and their constant production of feathers, dust, and droppings, scattered in great part by the breeze. I wanted to study that color more closely, but meanwhile told myself that if anyone saw me stopping repeatedly to look back, he or she might think I'd been seized by a kind of fear of or obsession with birds. No matter where I am or what I do, I cannot free myself from the thought that I'm being observed and judged by others, nor from my frustrating inability to imagine the nature of their evaluations.

As I approached the open section of the park, which from my perspective promised to be fairly large, I could more clearly make out splotches of color that represented people in various postures and situations: they were sitting on benches, walking, or lying in the sun and under isolated trees. A large fountain in the center sprayed jets of water all around, creating a mist that blurred the surrounding space like a vaporous, unmoving cloud. When I reached the tree-lined mall and got closer to the fountain, I saw bougainvilleas again, purple like those in the circular garden, spread out here and there over a much greater space. As perhaps might be imagined, I instantly felt a bond with the few people walking there, since they were sharing in that halfheartedness, even lethargy, of mine toward walking in parks, which I referred to earlier as well. So I began to think about how long I've been taking walks. Years, decades. And if I live significantly longer I could keep on adding, because one thing I'm sure of is that I'll never stop. But despite this great amount of walking, however, no walk has provided me with any genuine revelation. In my case it's not as it was in the past, when walkers felt reunited with something that was revealed only during the course of the walk, or believed they had discovered aspects of the world or relationships within nature that had been hidden until then. I never discovered anything, only a vague idea of what was new and different, and rather fleeting at that. I now think I went on walks to experience a specific type of anxiety, one that I'll call nostalgic anxiety, or empty nostalgia. Nostalgic anxiety would be a state of deprivation in which one has no chance for genuine nostalgia. There may be various reasons for the block. If I'm going to explain it, I have to tell the story of my borrowed ideas, which I'm full of—I say "borrowed," but I'm not suggesting I don't have full rights to them, on the contrary . . .

One of these ideas, among the first I assimilated so thoroughly as to make it my own, was the idealization, initially during the Romantic Era, then the Modern, of the long walk. There must have been something wrong with me, because at the point at which I should have chosen a way of life for my future, I found nothing persuasive. From early on I've felt unequal to any kind of enthusiasm:

incapable of believing in almost anything, or frankly, in anything at all; disappointed beforehand by politics; skeptical of youth culture despite being, at the time, young; an idle spectator at the collective race for money and so-called material success; suspicious of the benevolence of charity and of self-improvement; oblivious of the benefits of procreation and the possibilities of biological continuity; oblivious as well of the idea of following sports or any variety of spectacle; unable to work up enthusiasm for any impracticable profession or scientific vocation; inept at arts or at crafts, at physical or manual labor, also intellectual; to sum up, useless for work in general; unfit for dreaming; with no belief in any religious alternative while longing to be initiated into that realm; too shy or incompetent for an enthusiastic sex life; in short, given such failings, I had no other choice but to walk, which most resembled the vacant and available mind.

To walk and nothing but. Not to walk without a destination, as modern characters have been pleased to do, attentive to the novelties of chance and the terrain, but instead to distant destinations, nearly unreachable or inaccessible ones, putting maps to the test. I laughed when someone would tell me a city was too large. And laughed as well if they told me it was too small. A city has one size, a fact known only to the person who walks it aimlessly, for all the world like a curious dog when it's strayed and lost its bearings, but isn't hungry or lonely yet. Here lies the blurry distinction between the cities' homeless and walkers such as me. One peers into a world where few, but definitive, rules divide people according to their street conduct and how long they remain there. I would often think . . . What do I want to find? A glimpse of the tramp's life, made up of nothing but fear and instant opportunism; or some old Modernist ideal that posited the long walk as the basis for a new urban religion. It's too confused and I'm not sure . . . That's why I've kept on walking, out of insecurity and a lack of convictions, as if walking were the ultimate experience I could offer to the ruined landscape I move through, with strength neither to overcome it nor destroy it.

As I said, the other walkers in the park—colleagues, as it were, in these adventures and private sorrows—had scattered themselves out across the greenswards and the vast, gleaming concrete esplanades, near-white with reflections from the bright sky, that dominated the alameda. The visitors, randomly grouped this way, seemed to accentuate the geometrical order of the area, rather than disrupt it. Despite the differences in their ages—they ranged from breastfeeding infants to the elderly infirm—each of them exuded that air I referred to earlier, at once absent and absorbed, self-abandoned, the sign, according to my criterion, of genuine familiarity with a park, and with all places generally. The young people were the most sociable, and a few solitary individuals carried their own maté kits, from which every so often, pensively, they'd take a long pull, at least that's how it seemed to me, or perhaps they were merely keeping the straw between their lips and forgetting to take a sip.

As everyone knows, Brazilian maté gourds are large; they'd be difficult to conceal if anyone was inclined to do so. Most difficult to hide, though, is the thermos—essential to all those who use a maté gourd, large or small. I headed for a bench that stood next to the fountain. Let's say that from the opposite side no one was able to see me through the jets of water and the cloud of mist mentioned earlier. Before taking a seat on the bench, I stood contemplating the panorama around me and all the while a fairly lengthy silence prevailed, unusual for that setting—even I noticed that—and I wondered if I were participating in a sort of collective trance, which included all the people and activity in the vicinity, or whether, on the contrary, I was suffering from a mental lapse, or was simply dreaming it. Whatever the case, I sat down, and a moment later took a deep breath; when I let it out, for an instant, and without knowing why, perhaps as a result of the cloud a very short distance away from where I sat, I briefly imagined I was invisible, or in hiding, and that an unaccustomed gift, or power, was allowing me to look without being seen. I put the map in my backpack, took out the book I had with me (it was a novel I'd been carrying around only a short while; I'd started reading it on the trip just before I arrived and hadn't had either the chance or the desire to go on with it since then), and became so engrossed in contemplating the water and the spaces around it that I felt omnipotent, as if a random but well-intended force had bestowed a gift upon me: I myself was dissolved in the mist that surrounded the fountain and could verify that my sight adjusted, in this way, to any situation: it could discern the indiscernible, catalog the invisible, uncover the hidden . . .

An old man was coming slowly toward where I sat, and only when he paused a short distance off did I realize he was going to sit down beside me without saying a word. No empty benches seemed to be left in the shade; and he was leaving the vast sun-scorched area as if emerging from a danger zone, with halting step, but content to have reached safety. His approach displeased me, as did his very materialization, which I took for a sign of hostility or, at the very least, an interruption. I realized immediately, however, that the intruder was most probably myself, and that this man in all likelihood walked every afternoon to a spot he now saw occupied by me. It wouldn't be the first time, I thought. I remembered other situations, of course, minor reversals of fortune lying dormant in the recesses of my memory. For instance, I was once, briefly, in a European city known for its splendid lake and venerable canals. I happened to be, quite literally, admiring the lake and strolling along the adjacent park. One of those German cities bombed in the Second World War, destroyed and then, with obsessive attention to detail, rebuilt to be just as they once had been. A while back I met a woman who, alongside her mother, took part in that rebuilding as a child; she told me about the women's brigades, made up of women of all ages, who'd worked on it. In particular, she remembered her work assignment: she had to move the remains of bricks from one corner—or what was left of it—to another, so as to sort the bricks that were still useful, and set aside the pieces too small to be usable. The few men who were present gave directions to the older women in accordance with some oversized specs and blueprints they were incessantly opening their arms wide to consult. Anyhow, this city now seemed far too impeccable to me, as on the whole German cities do; it proclaimed that there had never been a war, much less such widespread devastation. I recalled the stories of that long-ago little girl as I walked through the park. It was just past noon, and from where I stood I could observe the busy avenue and the orderly flow of cars. Some swans from the colony that had settled on the lake—the only visible fauna, as far as I know, besides the underwater variety—swam up to anyone who approached the water's edge, doubtless hoping for something to eat. And when they received nothing they would bury their heads and the full length of their long necks in the water, to hide their failure, I suppose, or to look for something in its depths.

A friend who was living in the city at the time had warned me that the swans devoured anything they came across, even the most rotten and foul-smelling stuff. In his view, the birds' voraciousness contradicted the bucolic image the lake was intended to project.

When I saw the swans anxiously courting me, never letting me out of their sight, I recalled his remark. Because of it I found them so unpleasant that I had to retreat to a path several dozen meters away that led to an avenue that encircled the lake. From that point on the path, one saw the surface of the water as a great metallic expanse. People who passed by this spot were either taking a short cut to a nearby railway station, which at that midday hour didn't attract many passengers, or were headed downtown and would have to go around the station on their way. Having nothing better to do, I sat on a bench and gazed at the skyline beyond the lake. I held the book I'd brought along for the day, which, as usual, didn't interest me, and which therefore I had no desire to open. I preferred to admire, as I said, the metallic expanse of the lake, despite its failure to glisten.

From that distance one could recognize the swans only by their sinuous necks, like ghostly shapes whose blurred silhouette concealed a secret or a promise to be revealed in the future, or in the present if the circumstances were different. All the time, though, my thoughts kept returning to an object I'd seen that morning in a shop near my friend's home. While I awaited him for our early breakfast, as we had arranged, I walked along the avenue browsing in shop windows. A wristwatch in one of the windows instantly caught my eye. Its case was black and its face white, this in itself didn't distinguish the watch from the rest; but what was unique was that it ran in reverse: the hands moved counterclockwise. This oddity, which I otherwise would have deemed irrelevant, since it turned the watch into a kind of toy or curiosity, became in this instance a coincidence charged with meaning. For various reasons, my visit to this German city confronted me with a particular point in time; it was a journey to the past, and in part, to a form of the past that indirectly belonged to me. On one hand, a good number of years had passed since I'd seen my friend, and being in his company now was causing me to relive, unexpectedly, and with who knew what outcome, several memories from an era we both had left well behind us; and on the other, ever since the train crossed the Belgian border, my apprehensions regarding this country, Germany, connected with the elimination of a good part of my family during the Holocaust, had been barely palpable, and still worse, were on the contrary being transmuted into a dulled sensation of guilt and frustration.

I'd heard so many stories about panic attacks, acute anguish, and nervous crises experienced by Jewish travelers upon arrival in Germany that it troubled my conscience not to feel what the post-Holocaust common sense now seemed to call for at the very least, that is, a kind of suppressed rage at all Germans, and every German, while at the same time at nobody in particular, at a community of people who'd supposedly settled into the most insulting indifference; and it frustrated me that the possibility of my experiencing a clear and direct emotion had been blocked—as was always the case, and still is, with me—an inhibition I'd believed would be overcome at a juncture so intimately fraught as my being in Germany. So the discovery of the watch stood out as a sign, or indeed, was a certain kind of symptom that had now materialized: I had found an object I related to the obstacles of my situation. In part my own, personal past, and in part that of my family, that unique zone where history was linked to a zone of my own identity, came together here. In the face of this, the reverse watch thus combined the ambiguity and the indifference with which reality speaks as it advances in its unbridled race toward the future. The watch epitomized the contradictory voice of objects, often more conspicuous and allusive than the human voice; it moved forward, like all instruments that measure time, and yet simultaneously said the opposite since it appeared to move backwards.

I imagined the watch on my wrist and thought of how long it would take to get used to reading the time that way, the questions I'd be asked, and so on. I especially imagined how others would react, that they'd regard the watch as yet another unequivocal sign of my tendency toward moderate extravagance, or, I should say, a mediocre extravagance, so timid as to hardly be verifiable. I also imagined my relatives after this trip to Germany, a sort of advance guard anxious for commentaries and impressions, for stories of panic attacks and scenes of ethnic or cultural shock; and I particularly imagined my nephew and niece, fascinated by the watch and eager to possess it, one of the few anachronistic talismans offered by the modern world, I thought. And lastly I imagined a certain moment in old age, a transcendent scene, the night of the legacy: I would give the reverse watch to my nephew or my niece, a sort of secret handshake marking my abstruse passage through the world, and he or she would keep it as a proof and a symbol, the side of me that would remain with them; the half-distant, fairly alien uncle who had once drawn near, almost at the end, believing it was forever, with that sentimental gesture and that odd device.

I have two prized objects to hand down: my grandfather's cigarette lighter, and my father's ivory binoculars. Besides these, nothing I own ever belonged to anyone else. I haven't thought yet about whether I'll give both objects to one of them or one to my nephew and the other to my niece. I'd have a problem if there were three of them: even if I tried, the share could never be equal. If I had bought that German watch—I doubt it would have been Chinese back then—I'd have something for a third. But at that moment, as

I sat in the park beside the lake, I imagined myself having bought it, so that I had three gifts. The reverse watch pointed to the past, that would be the best legacy, a caveat that we should always look behind us so as to discover our own nature. And what's the point of knowing our own nature, the nephew or niece might ask. To hide it, I'd reply; to subjugate it, which is impossible, and to hide it, so as to believe we've left it behind, etc. To delude ourselves, and move forward.

The watch, I mean, represented a course of action. I recall how its high price impressed me that morning, and I was unsure whether it was due to the watch's quality or its rarity. Of course, if such an object was to be distinctive, it had also to be a bit expensive, because if it were cheap that would declare its uselessness. I could say a great deal more about the cigarette lighter and the binoculars, in particular I could say that they, unlike the watch, are objects that offer no lessons, despite being excellent heirlooms. A family such as mine, which came out of that void an ocean away, knowing nothing of its history beyond a few decades back, will suddenly in the future have tangible proof of an almost deep past, in objects that will condense the history of individuals and bodies. It could be amazing. And I thought, all thanks to these three objects. In my younger days as a smoker I used to use my grandfather's cigarette lighter. From time to time, I still use my father's binoculars, but mostly I periodically open the leather case, which over time has become so thin it's like dried-out paper about to crumble. I take out the binoculars, heft them and inspect them, peer through them, turn the central wheel to focus, and finally stow them away in their case. Curiously, over time this inspection has turned into a ritual that has nonetheless forgotten its referent; I mean, my memories of my father are by now largely distant; I don't think of him when I take out the binoculars, except as an idea. Not as a living person, with a voice and a certain warmth but, rather, as a figure that person has occupied ever since he abandoned, as they say, this world.

For reasons of chronology, the cigarette lighter has been with me far longer. And, compared with the binoculars, it has offered a greater range of useful possibilities, at least in my case; and so, as I said, in my days as a smoker I used it quite a bit. I always marveled at its mechanism, which for want of a better word I called automatic; it was my fear of breaking this mechanism by my heavy use that finally persuaded me to stop using it. For years it's been stored in the depths of a cardboard box, along with old bus tickets and souvenirs that were essential in their day. Now the only important thing in the box is this lighter. Its mechanism consists of a button on the upper-left-hand side; that is, it's made for right-handed people. Cradling the lighter in your hand, you press the button with your thumb and the top part, a lid in the shape of a cylindrical tube, suddenly flips up. As the lid opens, a cogwheel connected to the hinge strikes the flint, creating a spark that lights the wick. A left-hander could use it, of course, but he or she would have to get used to the inconvenience of the flame igniting inward, not outward, or would have to hold the lighter gingerly and press the button in a rather awkward position.

As I said, for years I took a ridiculous pride in this oddity; from an early age, though I didn't fully realize it at the time, I was half-aware that it was an object to be handed down. My grandfather was notorious for smoking like a chimney, as they used to say. Every morning the local tobacco shop would deliver a carton of filterless cigarettes. I was in first grade, and could verify that the carton was almost the same size as the 100-piece boxes of chalk I sometimes saw at school. One Saturday, I recall, I was present during a conversation between my grandmother and the owner of the tobacco shop, who pressed her not to allow my grandfather to smoke at such a rate. Either my grandmother was incapable of controlling him, or was so unconcerned that it made no difference to her. But that's another story; in the end my grandfather continued to get hold of his cigarettes and to smoke in a sort of domestic exile in which, I suppose, as is frequently the case, the tobacco kept him company.

The surface of both sides of the lighter was uniformly striped, with an elegance that to me recalled Art Deco. I've seen pewter or perhaps silver-plated cigarette cases with a similar scoring on their cover, a motif, I've always thought, that seeks to imitate the futuristic cladding of the early twentieth-century. Down the center of the same side of the lighter as the button, you can see a small rectangular plate, obviously intended to be engraved as one pleases: with a name, initials, or a date. Inevitably for someone as hazy as its former owner, the plate on this lighter is blank. A missing inscription that accentuated the lighter's availability, or its mysteriousness in any case, because as is true for nearly all manufactured objects, a simple change of hands can send a supposedly well-planned transfer awry, leaving nearly no trace.

I don't want to generalize, but that is the true condition all objects force on us, not only manufactured ones: that of concealing the history they have witnessed, in complete silence. With some effort on one's part, they can be made to speak; an entire industry has sprung up around making what's silent speak. For a time I thought that was why literature existed, books in general, or indeed, the written word itself in any form: the written word confronts what exists so as to get it down. Afterward I stopped attaching so much importance to the matter, which I recall from time to time, on occasions like this, when I'm reconstructing my relationship to some object.

Such were my thoughts in that great German city. I was thinking more about myself, obviously, than about the number of things in all likelihood buried beneath that urban perfection. As long as these weren't visible, they didn't matter to me. I thought of the reverse watch and of the valuable lesson it would provide a niece or nephew, and one of their children, and so on through subsequent generations. The perennial lesson of looking behind you, and the irrefutable proof of coming from a specific place. I was sitting on a bench gazing every now and then at the lake, where I could make out the swans in profile as they prowled the lake's edge, fishing—probably, as I said—for something to eat, and every so often I looked out at the distant avenue besides which the aforementioned railway station stood. I was absorbed in thoughts that had no resolution and were somewhat brief, mere formulations. For instance, I thought: "So far from home . . . I would have never imagined being here"; and it also occured to me: "At night, when they turn on the ornamental lights and the rest of the water jets in the lake, everything will look different"; etc. The unceasing jets at the lake's center signaled, in that sense, the continuity both of one's thoughts and of the water, like two inseparable elements . . .

I was lost in these ruminations when all at once two women stopped in front of me and began waving their arms at me. I didn't realize it at first, but they wanted me to leave the bench to them so that they could eat lunch. Each carried a paper-wrapped packet with her lunch, and one woman also carried two plastic forks. I imagined they were probably foreigners, like me but less so, though in any event from a different place. They didn't speak to me in German—in truth they hardly spoke to me at all—but they managed to communicate everything with gestures. They wore clothes from another era, from which I gathered that they were from somewhere in Eastern Europe, perhaps not far away. Poland or Ukraine, who knows. And, as one often notices in cities, the difference was visible in their skin as well, because at first glance one saw in them the harsh weather of rural life. I can't say that these women were brusque, but I do remember they were lacking in the often equivocal kindness one finds in European cities.

They were clear and concise. I could say nothing in defense of my sitting there in meditation, and so I sketched a bow of my head that would hide my embarrassment, by way of farewell, and walked away without looking back, blending in with pedestrians who were in a rush to cross at the green light. At times nowadays I look through the photos I took on that trip, and I see the magnificent lake, and there's my friend, leaning his elbows on the balustrade of a bridge, and beyond him a group of swans near the shore. Several of them have buried their imposing bills and their heads in the water, taking up a position that seems precautionary, as if they preferred to hide and not have their picture taken. Further in the background, though, there's a solitary swan that, more radically, is making its escape and is well into take-off. I see its half-spread wings, which seem to be coming apart at the joints, its neck stretched forward to the limit, and its feet touching the lake as if it were running on the surface. The creature leaves behind evidence of its steps, bursts of water that explode as waterdrops and turbulence which disappear little by little, as the photo shows: the initial splashes have dispersed and are about to vanish.

When I got to my feet and turned the bench over to the two women, neither conveyed any gratitude by word or gesture, nor even any acknowledgement, not even a glance; and so I felt vaguely annoyed at their shooing me away like a bothersome animal, a swan for instance. I guessed that they probably ate their lunch on that bench every day and always arrived at the same hour, getting together to meet and speak of their families and their memories of the East, and that I had played the role of a quickly remedied setback. Yet another of those visitors who occasionally erred and sat down on their bench . . .

So I wondered whether the old man approaching me now, in flight from the sun with his last reserves of strength, wasn't the customary occupant of the bench. In that case, I could say: in the south of Brazil there's an old man who every afternoon sits on the same bench in the shade. Just before he took a seat, he greeted me with a nod that for a moment seemed dismissive, though it sufficed to make me forget my displeasure. And after he settled in as far away from me as possible, on the opposite end of the bench, he took a deep breath and began to untie his shoes. He didn't take them off at first, but merely loosened them. Then he stretched his legs, rested his hands over his stomach, and appeared to sleep. A bit later, with a deft motion of his heels, he did what was necessary to take off his shoes. What with the muffled shouts that arrived from the distance, the trill of the birds, the constant hum of the bustling city and, in particular, the turbulent fountain with its endlessly spurting water, I was astonished to be able to hear my benchmate let out a sigh.

Early that same morning, shortly after leaving the hotel, I'd been strolling along the river, on the other side of town. The day was just getting started, and the traffic on the avenue next to the river seemed unusually sparse, so sparse that the timing of the traffic lights caused the few cars or buses to travel in herds, one after the other, as if they were families of vehicles. In the intervals a silence would fall, during which one could look at the water, at the opposite bank, sharply defined and wild, and cheer up on feeling that a moment from the past had been slipped into the present. It's odd, I thought, how one abandons the future and seeks to recover the past. But recover wasn't the word. I didn't want much, barely a glimpse. Any trace I could discover would be a revelation to me, from the fragile, petrified branch of a fallen tree to a landscape remembered from childhood, though I might never have been there. As is perhaps becoming clear, everything in Brazil was pushing me into the past. Into a hazy past, pre-cerebral, which clouded my perceptions and affected my judgment, demolishing it.

During one of the lulls in traffic, while I was leaning against the railing of a broken-down iron pier that jutted out over the river, I had a sort of revelation. The past, like myself an itinerant, acted like a meander, with no precise, let alone predetermined, direction, which could absorb all our free time, or might simply leave us cold. What's more, like a sleepwalker who's forgotten his dream and doesn't know whether he's awake. I was in the process of turning into one of its perhaps exemplary victims, and consequently ending up bogged down in sterility. I was just then presenting the first symptoms, I thought: the absence of a desire to know. I had the city at my back, each particle of it like a cell of an immense country, and nevertheless, there I was, stuck on the far end of the ruined pier trying to elicit anything at all from the dense, hazy bush on the opposite bank. This feeling, I can now state, wouldn't leave me for the rest of that day, or on the ones that followed.

I left the old pier—I recall how the hanging structure trembled with each new footfall, as it had when I'd first stepped onto it—and set off along the path beside the river. Beyond the sidewalk, and before the avenue next to the river, was a spacious parking lot, most likely full on the weekends. In the distance you could make out a group of people, some fifty meters ahead, who seemed to be waiting for more people to arrive, though of course I couldn't be sure; and behind me, maybe thirty meters back, I'd seen a married couple, or simply a couple, who were preparing to open their refreshment stand. I point this out because of what I'm about to explain; I mean, I saw no one at all in my immediate vicinity. Nonetheless, as I walked along I was able to hear, during one of the breaks in traffic, what sounded like a long, resonant slurp.

A familiar noise, for me: somebody could be drinking maté. I took a closer look and noticed, a few meters off and almost parallel to me, a shuttle bus, the kind used at airports, with its door half-open. From where I stood, I could see two bare feet in plastic flip-flops peeking out from beneath the door. I immediately backed away, as discreetly as I could, stepping a few paces away from the riverbank, so as to see the person hidden behind the door. I could be sure of attracting no one's attention, but I moved with the caution of a spy, an indecisive voyeur. I then circled nonchalantly around and indeed found the driver, seated on a folding chair, drinking maté. Though I had no way of verifying it, I understood him to have spent the night in the bus, at least that's how it seemed to me at first sight. From his position he could see only part of the river, in the lee of the tall chimney of an old utility plant that had once supplied power to the city.

I remembered that loud slurp as I thought about the old man's sigh. The strange coincidence of having detected the two. My benchmate fell into an apparently deep sleep, threatened now and then by a nervous startle, something like a reflex action or an outright tic, or by sense-related incidents, it seemed to me, like swatting away an insect or flinching at a surprise or reacting to an unexpected gap in the continuous noise. I noticed we were sitting under a bougain-villea, similar to the ones you could see in the park's open spaces; owing to the symmetry of that particular area—its broad esplanade flanked by a double file of benches and trees, and adorned with parterres that were small, taking into account the dimensions of the whole, composed of privet hedges and flowers laid out with a care for balance, to which must be added the fountain as the crowning glory and epicenter of the geometric endeavor—for a moment I thought that the two of us sat on the opposite side, beyond the fountain, under those other bougainvilleas, not this one.

The clouds of mist and water drops filling the air didn't make for clear sight, but I was able to distinguish my own self, sitting with my legs crossed, the small backpack on my lap, and I saw the old man too, at the far end of the bench, to my left, resting or fast asleep, turning to good account the tranquility of the place and the afternoon. I could make out beyond us, some meters back, a group of people sitting on the grass, in what seemed a gathering of family or friends. From time to time one of them would get up to joke around with another, to tag him and then go running off, for instance, or to startle him, whatever. Now and again a man stretched his arms over his head, which caused him such evident pleasure that he decided to lie down on his back and pretend to be asleep. I could hear voices and bursts of laughter, at irregular intervals, of course. But what amazed me was that even though I could see them all on the far side of the fountain, beyond my companion and myself, I heard them as if their voices came from behind us, from where we were actually seated. Perhaps this was another effect of the place or, more precisely, of the mist created by the jets of water, which dissolved present time and distorted space; or it could have been a consequence of the symmetry. The present: until that afternoon I had rarely noticed the confused, and at times inconsistent, meaning of this word, to which we should add the sense of ambiguity it often possesses . . .

Beneath the circle of moisture, I imagined I could be the old man with his shoes off; and that thanks to this miraculous coincidence of time, place and circumstance, I was visiting myself from one extreme of the wide band called the present, to a still broader recess, vaguer and, as I put it before, more meandering, called the past. I had traveled to this park to call on myself, for instance, after having distributed my bequests. The worthy cigarette lighter, unengraved, to a nephew, the prized ivory binoculars to a niece, and the reverse wristwatch, to the youngest, a nephew, so that the lesson implicit in the mechanism would last the longest. At first I wasn't struck by the incongruity of handing down a watch which had never belonged to me. And when I realized my error, I chalked it up to confusion or to the absentmindedness that can afflict an older person, like my benchmate.

My nephew reacted with some discomfort. The watch was outlandish, but he failed to understand the symbolic or pedagogical importance I had wanted to give it. I pressed it on him unemphatically, in my way, that is, half-indifferent and a bit complacent, so as not to completely frighten him off from an idea that he might in the future, on reconsideration, accept; my lackluster style of arguing, however, undermined a good part of my argument, and aside from that I argued without conviction, as is normal for me anytime and anyplace. He was the youngest and he was the best. How to put it . . . the one who was most receptive and open, who wanted to know everything, to imbibe the world in every breath. The watch, in short, was a time machine that would allow him to connect to the past; not to visit it or glimpse it, just to connect. Not with the future, true; but who cares about the future if it arrives no matter what, I declared to a child for whom the past meant nothing. And to allay his distrust I offered him proof; it was so well-suited to connecting with the past that during a trip to the south of Brazil I happened to see myself in a park, taking a rest on a hot afternoon under a bougainvillea.

After I sat down on one end of a bench, I continued, I loosened my shoelaces, stretched my legs, and sighed in relaxation as I closed my eyes, ready to let myself be carried along for a time by the noises of the afternoon and the deep shade. A moment later I took off my shoes in the proper way, using my heels. And at that point I realized what was happening: the absentminded gentleman who was sitting on my bench, and who appeared to be thinking of nothing, was a representative from my past, a retrospective warning; that's why his mind was completely blank, at most he was pondering the challenges presented by hunger and his need for food that night, because the idea of going into a restaurant or a café alone tortured him, put his painful shyness to the test, and took up an unspeakable amount of time, a continuous present. This was in part a result of his endless walks whenever he was visiting a city, because he was afraid of going into any given place and being identified as an impostor or, more realistically, simply being treated badly for no reason at all.

When I awoke, everything was in its place. The old man let out a barely audible snore, which at times stretched into a sort of languid and seemingly definitive exhalation. A woman strolled slowly past in front of us, accompanied by her small dog. In a bag she carried the maté kit I'd seen her using as she sat on one of the benches in the sun. She strolled by, as I said, and as she did so she proffered us a look of complicity, as if she sought to fraternize with the park's habitués. That may have applied to the old man, but not to me. The dog cast a similar glance at us, with no need to check its owner's expression first to see what she did. It's hard to describe the sensation of a task well done that assailed me at that moment: I believed that I'd found the key to a certain inner life of the park. In a few hours of walking and contemplation, I achieved what I'd so rarely managed before, even in places I'd lived in for months or years: to be considered a denizen of the place. From my point of view, the sole reason this took place originated in one of the terrain's most outstanding virtues: its natural division into specific areas, which led to one's forgetting about the other areas entirely. It had happened to me in the aviary, in the labyrinth-garden, and it was happening to me now by the fountain on the alameda. Despite their lack of physical boundaries, these were well-circumscribed spaces, confined and self-sufficient, which had a world effect, though there must be a better term for it, an exemplary, hard-earned balance between landscape and atmosphere, with an obvious impact on people's powers of perception.

The effect of that layout was a deceptive appeal, because at first you believed you were in a park, while in fact you were in several at once, though in none of them, however, did you see that flashiness associated with the most widespread and predictable ideas of natural beauty. It was a park on the edge of extinction and oblivion, that was obvious, but it lived on thanks to its invincible beauty and to the wisdom that had designed it to endure in times of destruction. The breeze shifted every now and then, bringing minuscule drops from the fountain my way, which nonetheless didn't soak me, but rather refreshed me like dew. In a bit I would be getting up and resuming my walk; I had known that before I'd made my decision. The powerful jets of water competed with one another to go the highest, and some of them, those which because of a defect or a deflection at their base veered sideways, traced a parabola that was hard to make out when the jets crossed each other, or when they reached their highest point, known as the apex I believe, and began to descend.

Through the spray of water I saw the bougainvillea on the other side of the esplanade. I'm not exaggerating when I mention the curious refraction of its brilliantly colored petals, deep red, as I said before, which as they became smudged like a still life in an Impressionist landscape, faded, were less strident, more opaque, and strangely, thanks to the watery effect, these same petals became more tangible, as if their natural adornment had overwhelmed them and the water particles and mist sought to correct this excess. I sat like that for a while, in wonder at the workings of the fountain. Its circular basin was, logically, full of water, near overflowing. It was odd to see how a boiling effect was created—I know no better way of describing it—a consequence of the thousands of drops of water striking the surface. For a moment it seemed to me that the jets of water, launched up from the widest variety of places and at random, and yet with the purpose of creating an illusion of freshness and turbulence, shot into the air not as jets, I mean, not as water forcefully expelled and sent in a predicted direction, but instead as traces of dotted lines marking out a journey. The water wasn't flowing, in reality someone had drawn it, just like the fountain—a stone grey made with soft graphite—and the esplanade, too, had been drawn somewhat lighter than its physical version, as the trees had been with their various intensities, the patches of shade beneath or between them, and also the people, alone or in groups, who'd been sketched as well in the most schematic or typical poses to adopt in a park. Even the water drops, whether the ones that exploded in splatters on the surface, or the lightest, most volatile, nearly vaporized one, were all, thanks to its display of minutiae, represented in the drawing.

Anyhow, nothing in that picture caught my attention more than the flow of the water, because it was the only object that appeared as a sign. And that inconsistency, or abstraction, compared to the veracity of the other components—which were in keeping with their natural proportions and with the verifiable nuances of light—made the representation of the jets more authentic, because in this way they proved double, or bifronted. It was a symbol, that is, the flow of water had an added materiality at the same time it lacked one. Was it water or was it a different element? Because in all likelihood an old route was being shown, or simply a prediction: the place through which the water jets ought to pass.

As might be readily expected, after having this thought I began to imagine a world made up of dotted lines, the indecisive sketch of its contours, the design of its relationships. Just as with the water, one could trace sounds, physical trajectories, material changes and the passage of time. The line denoted the relationship between objects, which could be of the same nature or not. But naturally, since this was a physical representation, each connection lingered on, permanently drawn on the paper, superimposed on earlier or later ones, creating the "fountain" effect I mentioned before: a weft of dotted lines that crisscrossed, and whose arcs ended up a bit tangled, delineating a complex skein; not illegible, with some effort, just slightly chaotic. And in that denseness I found a kind of dramatic consistency, as much in the most immediate, theatrical sense, as in the tragic sense: the fatuous display of the real as the triumph of destiny.

I don't know what came over me. This interpretive behavior or feeling so conquered me that when I saw a distant hiker pouring his maté, I immediately reconfigured the stream of water, which was of course invisible to me in the distance, as a dotted line that dropped from the lip of the thermos making a curve. The line I restored had an extra feature: it bulged a bit exaggeratedly, was rounder and more pot-bellied than in reality, the better to stand out. The addition of the curve, the paunch, stood for the price of becoming visible and, in the process, acquiring consistency. That's why I'm not exaggerating when I say that for me that afternoon in the south of Brazil the world was transformed. From one single and simultaneously inconsistent place, the universe reorganized itself at will, according to relationships that were always visible. In the middle of the day, what was visible was radically unsettled, or better still, it appeared in a form until that moment wholly unknown, at least not by me . . .

I decided to leave the bench and resume my walk. I looked over to where the old man was sleeping: he hadn't moved, other than swatting the occasional insect. I looked at his hands, folded together over his belly, and only then did I realize that the book I'd taken out when I sat down was still in my lap; at one point I'd opened it, surely like those readers on trains or in waiting rooms who interrupt their reading, look up, sit there rapt in something, and don't start reading again for quite some time. I had fallen into one of those reveries, I realized now, and I also knew I wouldn't return to the book for the rest of the day, or even attempt to.

The alameda that served as a stage for the monumental fountain opened out impressively; it must have been a hundred-odd meters long and some thirty meters wide. It offered two parallel walkways, which ran its entire length, crossed every few meters by transverse paths. Between the walkways was a narrow watercourse, half-concealed by the paths, beneath which you could make out small cascades or locks through which the water travelled on its way from the fountain. Trees surrounded the area with an equal denseness. Given the land's gentle downward slope, from its topmost point the alameda seemed more extensive than it really was; but above all it looked like a startlingly geometric clearing amid the dense plant life, because wherever one looked one could make out, under the green of the trees, shadowy masses, spaces at first sight overgrown and impenetrable. I headed off down one of the walkways. On my right I could distinguish something like an Oriental garden, or strictly speaking Japanese, with a great number of stones and promontories, shallow waterfalls, and very narrow canals that connected two ponds that were equally diminutive, given the scale of their surroundings. From a distance I saw too, a number of sculptures, of a Buddhist sort, solid and dark gray, which because of the contrast these made with the innocent wooden bridges scattered here and there gave the garden a mien that was somber, even threatening, rather than harmonious.

Toward the left of the alameda, in the other area, stood a dense forest, broken at times by a few small clearings where they'd set out rustic tables for snacking or picnicking, or both things at once. I spied three men sitting around one of these tables, devoting themselves to what appeared to be a game, dominoes or cards, I couldn't tell. Needless to say, I had reason to doubt my first impressions; the dominoes may have been a misperception, a mere whimsical transposition of images from the past, of those facts, perennial in their way, that alight in one's memory and lead a furtive life there, surface occasionally and are then obliterated until their next appearance. I recalled a fairly hot summer, in another city. The doors and windows in the neighborhood open day and night, the neighbors avoiding the insides of their houses, etc. I remembered the dry slap of the dominoes on the tables set up in the street or in courtyards and gardens. Sessions that lasted for hours. Several games were most likely being played, one after the other, but as a result of the repetition and the unrelenting heat, these turned into a single game that never ended. As a background to the slapping of the tiles, you heard the murmur of voices; it was the conversation that flowed on, independent of the game, to be interrupted every now and then by long intervals of silence, or, depending on the ups and downs of the play, by a volley of shouts that died away almost instantly. And it wasn't just one table, there were hundreds spread out all over the neighborhood, from which the sound of the slapping Bakelite would carry distinctly, although that didn't matter, because given the similarity of the sounds, one could reconstruct those that were the faintest, determine their true source, and above all, their true color.

I went on considering the waves of sounds that ran like currents and seemed to work by emulation. I would hear them far off, then near, I'd feel how they enveloped me, little by little, then left me behind, their aftereffects slowly fading, and so it went, several times a day. I was capable of finding a poetry in that, but even to me, accustomed to being satisfied by so little, it seemed obvious. As is evident, I was growing gloomier and more fatalistic. Maybe that's why I thought it all too likely that the park would offer me no other varied or interesting things, though it's true that at that point in the afternoon—or more generally, in my life—I could no longer be sure of what I expected. I then decided to find the closest exit. I wanted to return along a different route and perhaps in this way come across some impressive monument, a grand gateway arch, the iconic portal, I don't know, because everything told me that I'd approached this park haphazardly, and it had therefore revealed itself to me slightly at random, failing to display its potential pathways or its perhaps intentional contrasts. On the whole, the same thing always happens to me. I set out from the margins or at the back doors, and that obviously determines how my impressions unfold. A handy example is the aviary, a place whose melancholy had surprised me, and which I had no desire to visit again; its melancholy would probably have moved me if I'd come across it in another sequence. I no longer remember the aviary in that way, but I was still under the effects of the place, the silence typical of caged creatures. And so, desiring to escape my own associations, I left the Buddhist area behind and took one of the side paths to the right, which led into the heart of the park, crossing it diagonally.

Once again I discovered on the ground the kind of earth with which I was by now familiar: a worn, near-pulverized gravel that resembled dirty, powdery sand. As I walked along, the noises from outside became more subdued and, apart from the predictable trillings and screeches now and then, a threatening silence prevailed. I don't know, to me the silence seemed the most visible proof of the falsity, or rather, the invention or manufacture, of an allegedly natural environment in the middle of a city. In the past, the park had probably been the site of farms or a post station, and then the city proceeded to engulf it. As I considered this, I realized that my dichotomous thinking was surfacing, because on the one hand, I love parks—or their funereal variant, cemeteries—and love them far more than any space devoted to natural habitat, or the alleged wild; but on the other, I never pass up a chance to slander them inwardly and verify, time and again, whenever I walk through them, the forced affectation that sustains them. At any rate, I suspect it's a useless battle, lost in advance: who would have any interest in what I think about parks, or better still, who would care what I think about anything. That's why, as I wrote before, I prefer untended parks, those that have been overtaken by neglect, because no one expresses any strong opinion about them and so they take on a still more autonomous life and, in that sense, presumably a more authentic one . . . Although of course, one can never know.

I now covered a long stretch on the diagonal path, where everything seemed to sleep, protected by the shade. It was an ideal path for walking aimlessly, indifferently. I kept seeing discarded candy wrappers and empty soft-drink cans on the ground. Some had been there for a long time, since they were weatherworn and had, in their own way, adapted to the colors in their surroundings. Because there were no benches or tables nearby, I surmised that on the weekends the path was heavily used. This made me want to know where it led to. From time to time I saw large trash cans, which were in any case brimming with papers and plastic bags. Not much else at all, besides the trees, the dry earth and the predominant shade. As had happened several times earlier on this outing, before long I spotted a light area toward the end of the path; and when I drew closer, some ten minutes later, I glimpsed a tableau that at first disturbed me, I don't know why: over there a good-sized, tranquil lake lay hidden, and from where I was approaching I could make out some unexpected, gigantic swans, stock-still and arrayed as if in regimental formation. As I drew nearer to the water and the scene grew better lit, I felt a mixture of wariness and wonder. Wariness owing to something quite primal, for which I realized I wasn't prepared: simply the size of those pedal boats in the shape of swans, which one associated more with some monstrous scale than with any idea of a replica or an amusement; and wonder because of the illusion of standing before an inanimate army, but one that seemed subject to a latent vitality, ready to awaken or be activated at any moment.

Once at the edge of the lake, amid thickets of greenery slanting out toward the water, which made for a certain difficulty in moving about, I could appreciate the grouping of swans in all its majesty and realism. They were some three meters tall, and despite their size, their bodies were perfectly proportioned, so that the stylized curve of their necks, famously praised by *modernista* poets, offered in these gigantic models a new and incontrovertible argument confirming it. The swans' verisimilitude extended even to minor details, such as the color of their bills, a brilliant orange verging on red, with one exception alone, whose bill was yellow, as in all likelihood occurs now and then in real life.

I don't know whether there are many species of swans; the one I'm familiar with was well represented there in any case: the so-called common swan, its body white and with its characteristic black mask rendering its face mysterious and each specimen seemingly identical to the rest. Nor do I know the name for the other group I saw there—most likely "white-faced swan," as simple as that—or perhaps these bordered dangerously on geese, since their only difference with the others was that they lacked a mask. Otherwise both types displayed a similar morphology. As the name indicates, the face of the white-faced swan exhibits no other color, apart from its bill, already mentioned, and its black eyes. The common swan, on the contrary, has a black cloth that rises from the base of its bill and stretches to cover its eyes. Described that way, it might seem to be a blindfold, but actually the mask is a bit wavy, and lends this variety a grace and dynamism that would otherwise be lacking without this whimsy, which at first strikes one as theatrical; also, toward the edges of its face, where one would expect its ears to be, if it had ears, were white openings that, I think, serve as eyes. Anonymous swans, we might imagine, attempting to pass incognito. The white-faced ones, on the other hand, have eyes that are two large black circles practically stamped on the skull.

Unlike almost all real swans, these were missing the caruncle, the fleshy outgrowth that grows at the base of their bill or on the head, and which, according to the field guides, tends to be erectile. It made sense that the swans lacked this accessory, since the only motion they could possibly simulate was by virtue of their pedals. I keep a photo in which they are arrayed in rows of six beside the boarding ramp, presumably moored. Beyond what I've just described, both their silence and their demeanor impressed me. These qualities might seem fantastical, but I knew I wasn't deceiving myself: one has to activate one's imagination to bestow life on these swans. It's the same with all inanimate things, we have to imbue them with life, but rarely do we find in the inanimate the type of silence or demeanor I now confirmed, nor to such a degree, as we seek, let's say, to fit them into some human scale. On Mondays the swans clearly didn't swim too much. If one wanted to endow them with life, one could believe it was owing to the fatigue that had built up over the weekend, their heaviest workdays. Nonetheless, despite their being, so to speak, parked that way, their lifelike side was borne out in the fact that they seemed ready to move at any minute.

The swans held two passengers and had dual sets of pedals, and on the left, similar to a car, was an semi-circular iron handlebar that made do as the rudder. I began to walk through the area, gazing at the lake through various arrangements of branches, or straight through the leaves of shrubbery. I stood in the shade, camouflaged in my own way by thickets that were nearly marshy, but curiously, everything else, the whole of the lake and the group of swans, but not me, seemed to be crouching, lying in wait for a certain signal.

71

The trees on the opposite shore of the lake were mirrored in the water, itself fairly green, but some patches of bougainvillea, lilac-colored in this case, also stained the lake's surface.

Probably because of their uniform alignment, but also the absence of any distinguishing marks—the exception being the yellow-billed swan—the swans at first seemed to lack individuality. But that first impression didn't last long, because when I'd walked onward, after taking a path that ran parallel to the shore, and reached the swan-rental facility, from which I could consider the creatures from their tail ends, I could see that a particular number had been painted on each. Closest to me were Nos. 24, 3, 15, and 11; Nos. 18 and 10 completed the row. I'm not sure why these details matter. In a park where the presence of humans had adapted itself so closely to the nature of the surroundings, these artificial models seemed mysteriously alive to me, in their own fashion eloquent and mute at once.

In order to go out on the dock and board a swan, you had to pay a rental fee at a narrow cement ticket booth with a Spanish-tile roof, a little like a chalet-style guardhouse. A sign atop it said PEDALINHOS and listed the prices for weekdays, weekends or holidays. The minimal rental was fifteen minutes, which may give the wrong idea about the true dimensions of the lake, since whoever wanted to go to the far end would need a good deal more time. It seemed unlikely to me that the swans were capable of getting up much speed, and a little later, when I saw one in action, I confirmed their slowness. The planking that doubled as a dock had pipe handrails painted green. To the left of it, more difficult to access by water—on foot you'd have to cross a narrow and perhaps risky plank—were moored other, more conventional boats, resembling open cars, which were clearly old, less graceful, and out of use for some time.

The lake is in the form of an elongated ellipse, and the *pedalinho* station stands just past the midpoint of one of its longer arcs. I could have easily circled the lake, following the path that paralleled the shore just a few meters from the water, but for some reason that I cannot now recall, maybe because I simply thought it was getting too late, who knows why, in the end I didn't. For almost its entirety the lake is surrounded by a strip of marshy land, low brush, and wild thickets. The *pedalinho* area stands next to an open plaza separated from the lake by still more plant life, through which one sees only intermittent reflections from the water, as if the lake were a mere intuition or belonged to a strange land.

The plaza next to the swans has as its epicenter a singularly beautiful Rationalist terrace, where there rises a structure that resembles a spinning top, with concentric circular platforms of uneven size, its Constructivist style similar to that of the small guardhouses described earlier, and painted the same antique yellow. I remember that the name of the architect, whose surname was German, appeared on one of the side walls of the circular structure. I walked around the small plaza, from which one could see the *pedalinhos* gleaming in the sun, especially their curves, that is, their flanks and their necks. I couldn't imagine the spot crowded with families or young people on a Saturday or Sunday, since it now seemed definitively overcome by solitude. At the entrance I'd seen the swan attendant, dressed in a shirt that was blue or sky-blue, and an ice cream vendor in a yellow-trimmed red uniform, who had left his cart standing in the middle of the path a few meters away. Both stood leaning against one of the short columns that guarded access to the plaza. Every so often the boat attendant would turn to check on the swans; a reflex action, no doubt, since he could be sure no one was around. Or perhaps he, too, also intuited the presence of a flickering or secret life in them and, prompted by this suspicion, kept a close watch.

At times a solitary walker, like myself, appeared on the path, or one with children, or perhaps a couple, whatever; but whichever it was, whether a regular or a first-time visitor, everyone walked around this section of the park as if gone astray, or on the whole with the slow step of someone groping his or her way through unsafe or unfamiliar terrain. Conceivably it was the deep shade, contrasting with the luminous reflections from the lake, that gave the area a cave-like air, the air of a place given over to secrets and surprises . . .

The attendant and the ice cream vendor kept at it, bonded, so to speak, by the advancing afternoon. They amused each other with an occasional exchange of brief, languid remarks, subsiding afterward into a long silence until their banter resumed. I was able to observe them very well when I sat down on the steps of the terrace to enjoy the tranquility of the place. They were wholly oblivious of me, it's even possible they never saw me, because I remember that as I passed by them I believed myself to be invisible, to the point of feeling a bit uncomfortable, since in such silence and solitude one doesn't expect to be ignored as if one didn't exist. In fact, I assumed, as is my habit, that under those circumstances a greeting was essential, and I half-sketched a wave as I walked through the entrance quite close to both of them, or I believe I did. But it was as if the wind had passed by. I won't deny I felt slightly mortified, if only fleetingly, since I'd forgotten all about it a moment later.

I'd like to know just when my need to greet others originated; there must have been a first time, because it wasn't always like this: I used to greet people just enough, in accordance with established conventions. Now for the most part I believe I still do a good job at it, though at times an imbalance arises. I venture a greeting, or am about to do so, then realize it's not reciprocated. The urge is irrepressible, and inconvenient too, because there's nothing more distracting than greeting someone, yet it's stronger than I am. I don't know what happens to other people, but in my case I think I know the cause: an uncontrollable mimetic urge impels me to greet. It's not that I want to be taken for a native, which would be impossible anywhere, but that I simply seek to be regarded as normal. I have an extremely basic idea of normality, related solely to what's superficial. But since for foreigners, what's superficial is always what's most visible, a greeting is the price you pay for wanting to be normal.

The ice cream vendor and the attendant weren't obliged to be normal, while I'm obliged to act it. I'm required to act normal, I repeat, in any place, including my own country. That's why what I described earlier happened, as I was diligently scrutinizing my map in the middle of the sidewalk, and all my doubts and worries briefly disappeared when I believed the street vendor was waving to me from the gutter, alongside the passing traffic. I returned his greeting and began walking toward him. And as I said, I felt tremendously embarrassed when I realized he was hailing another person to ask for help. Partly because of it, I turned my eyes back to the map, as if I were hiding, and kept on trying to make sense of it. I now replayed those events and was under the impression I'd undergone them a good while ago, not merely a few hours earlier; and furthermore, I was under the impression I'd experienced them in another situation, in another time scheme, and under other conditions. I don't know whether this may have been an effect of the park—most likely it was. Parks and long walks separate me from time and install me in a different dimension, an alternate one, obviously compatible with the true one, shall we say, or in any case with the regular one, isolated and at times autonomous as it may be.

For instance, from a certain distance I took part in the predictable development of that muted conversation between the two men, the swan attendant and the ice cream vendor, and despite there being nothing in their dialogue that in the least concerned me or aroused my curiosity, I recognized in the scene an essential act, a privileged and moving event which I was flattered, even proud, to have witnessed. It might sound a bit presumptuous, but that's how it was. Somewhat like my reaction to the landscape the ground often presents. It was a simple or forgettable conversation, a way of killing time; perhaps it wasn't a conversation at all, but for me it had a transcendent quality. I thought: the park, the harmonized light and shade, the lake, the manufactured nature, the world in miniature, the imitation of fauna, etc., and on top of that, the communication, whose possible simulation I had no reason to rule out, between two individuals. Never before had a dialogue seemed so essential to me. I don't mean that in dramatic terms, as something essential to resolving a conflict or a mystery, but rather in terms of its human significance, I don't know what to call it, metaphysical might perhaps be too much . . .

Anything, it seemed, could distract those two men, except myself, of course, and when I passed them again on leaving it was as if nothing had happened. My next destination was a building that rose in the distance, at one end of the lake, spacious and low-built, beneath the green canopies of the trees which framed it from behind. The lake was to my left, sheltered by the profuse greenery which seemed to seek to disguise or to conceal it. At one point I thought that in all likelihood that afternoon would be my only time in this place, and so I couldn't resign myself to the idea of not having another look at its waters. So I first went deep into the grass and then slipped through the stunted shrubs and trees by the shore. The water wasn't very clear, but a few carp were visible, and one or another turtle swimming with effort, slowly, apparently at risk of sinking, nothing but their diminutive head, like a small nut, bobbing on the surface.

In controlled lakes such as that one, you can analyze, or at least see, the vicissitudes of a well-regulated life. Turtles and fish swim in peace, it's hard to imagine anything threatening them. A life well-regulated so as to go on, oblivious of the struggle and adapted to its own, possibly unhappy, subsistence. These creatures, including the swans, could give me some kind of a lesson. I tried to see it clearly, but something hindered me; probably weariness. After a life devoted to thinking trivialities, weariness was my body's last protest, the cry for help, now nearly extinguished, which still contains some kind of hope. I don't want to be overly abstract, but at times weariness translates into longing. That's what I felt at that moment: a longing for the well-regulated life, and for what's foreseeable.

Most likely owing to my shadow as seen from underwater, and the hope for food it represented, a few fish swam up to me, followed by two or three turtles. I had nothing more to offer them than my bitter thoughts and a vague feeling of solidarity with their condition, a condition in which I recognized myself completely: if their lot had fallen to me, I would have been the most well-regulated of carp and the most predictable of turtles; I had nothing to offer them and yet they stayed there, without moving, drawing a semi-circle before me, hanging on my movements as if they made up an audience willing to watch me, with their own rules for positioning themselves and their own patience. Of course, I felt immediately called upon to do something. A writer always dreams of a real audience, and this was the most I could aspire to. Needless to say, I was tempted to give a speech or at least offer some brief disquisition. Because the realest audience is the one that understands the least, I mean, when it flaunts its deafness, or at least a bit of resistance, when it indicates our uselessness, etc.

That's why I immediately felt united to these people, if I can call them that, since I'd never manage to know how they'd receive my words, or if my words would affect them in any way. They were, therefore, an ideal alibi, because thanks to their incomprehension I would address the world, all the species of the universe and their own materiality. I began by explaining to them how I'd arrived there, my problems in finding that splendid park. The animals listened to me with reverence and didn't take their eyes off me; I'm not exaggerating when I say they seemed hypnotized by my story. The carp were motionless under the water, their unblinking eyes almost breaking the surface; the turtles, meanwhile, were paddling their feet to keep their heads afloat as their heavy bodies seemed on the verge of sinking. I ended up giving a speech in the least expected of places. I had never been especially interested in animals, apart from regarding them as companions in misfortune of a sort, though for disparate reasons, some unknown to me. That's why I now didn't know whether I should adopt an apologetic tone or disregard my former indifference toward them, imputing it to the passage of time or to a mere lack of communication. But, of course, I could have no idea, either, whether they expected any explanation on this matter from me.

I thought of presenting my impressions of the aviary, the stupefied, degraded birds killing time in their gigantic cages. I could tell them a bit about the uncoordinated strut of the peacock, which walked about the wide birdcage as if evading imaginary obstacles.

A reeling caused not only by the weight of its great, fanned-out tail—an operation for which I saw no reason besides its desperation at being caged—but by the presence of some fact or some condition nonetheless invisible to me. That is, I had more than enough to say about their comrades in the park, but of course they were in all likelihood uninterested in hearing my opinion about them, a situation with which they probably were quite well-acquainted. They perhaps wanted me to speak about myself, or about my own species, Argentines, males, human beings in general, or whoever my peers were. Maybe they expected a rhapsodic speech harking back to the past and which praised a harmonious, shared natural origin. All of that could have happened, but the fact is I chose not to continue beyond this point.

I found it impossible that this situation should be occurring, and nevertheless that's what was happening. We remained silent for a good while, in a sort of mutual contemplation. It may have only seemed so to me, but the carp and the turtles had taken on a supplicating mien. Their bodies swayed steadily in time with the water, corresponding to the gentle waves that reached the shore; and I was startled to verify that, despite their to-and-fro, they were able to keep their eyes fixed on mine, as if—the anxious thought occurred to me—they wanted to etch my face and my demeanor in their memory, in case we met again in the future. I understood it as a threat. The animal world continues to be fairly unknown, and I have no notion how they transmit experiences there. I wanted to cover my face with my hands to hide myself, and spy on them from between my fingers without their seeing me. Nonetheless they remained just the same, expectant. If someone had at that moment looked where I was standing, he would have thought it was a matter of a man weeping, a possibility which, when I tired of the position, made me feel like not lowering my hands: I feared I would find human eyes on me, surely anxious to discover some morbid detail or an explanation, perhaps the eyes of the attendant or the ice cream vendor, or those of a father bored with walking through the deserted park with his child.

Before this afternoon, I'd never wondered whether animals could be curious, like people. This situation made me see that the question was relevant, because my guests—note my vanity—never took their eyes off me. I knelt before the water as a means of getting out of the situation. My plan was to lift my hands suddenly from my face and give them a scare; once they'd been frightened off I'd go on my way as if nothing had happened. But it didn't work. I waited a short while, the silence growing predictably deeper, and then all of a sudden I threw open my arms, gave a shout, leaned still farther over the water, and attempted to make a scary face. The front rows of the orchestra didn't blink, as if each one of them had been sure of what to expect. Nothing was keeping me from turning my back on them and returning to the path, but we'd established a communication, and I didn't want to be the one to put an end to it. Finally the solution came from someone also natural to the lake. First I noticed the waters roiling, and my audience as well; afterward I found out it was caused by a swan passing, though making its way relatively slowly. On board rode a father with his daughter, or so I imagined.

When I met the eyes of the two passengers, I offered a greeting. But I noticed that they weren't so prepared for the situation, since the daughter kept looking at me impassively, while the father conveniently averted his eyes. I waited for them to move away a bit; they were heading for one of the far ends of the lake, where I had glimpsed the low-lying building. The swan was No. 15, it sported the number on its tail end painted shiny black, similar to the paint of its eyes. As I noted before, I had seen this specimen parked next to the boarding ramp, and now, meeting up with it again, I felt some solidarity with its condition. But as if it had been a signal, its entrance on the scene dispersed my audience, because when I looked at the water again, I found that the carp and the turtles had moved off. I managed to make out one lone turtle as it swam half-heartedly toward the middle of the lake.

It's one of the things that will always remain a mystery, and which no one believes when I mention it, of course. But it happened, and I've remembered it so truly that I can't manage to visit any park and its corresponding lake without reliving those feelings of perplexity I experienced when the carp and the turtles were observing me, as if they scrutinized me. What must they have thought of me? What do animals think of me, if they indeed think . . . I elected to return to the path that circled the lake to go on with my walk; I had the sensation of having been present at a part of an extended reality, though obviously minimal, reserved only for my private experience.

I don't ask myself those types of questions on a habitual basis, and when I do they refer to people: what do those who know me think of me, or rather, what must they think of me? I'm not referring to those closest to me, those who've known me for years and with whom I have a lasting bond. I worry about the opinion of the others, the half-acquaintances, if I can call them that, those who know me a bit, maybe only by sight, and to whom I'm relatively familiar, or on the contrary, relatively hazy and non-existent. It's a recurrent question, which otherwise doesn't always make me as curious, perhaps because of its sporadic nature, yet it's one I take up every so often as proof of my own existence, or rather, my physical permanence in the world.

In one way, the question acts as a private beginning of fiction, or rather, as a beginning of private fictions: I see myself through the improbable eyes of people for whom, quite possibly, I don't exist in actual reality and in whose minds I'm no more than a blip. Here are the facts: that afternoon in the south of Brazil, it was November, the month of my birthday. When I noticed the coincidence I realized that I'd assigned to turtles and carp the thoughts that each year visited me with astronomical punctuality. The month was even well along—more than half over, only a few days left. As is evident, the occasion served as an invitation to meditate on the passage of time, on the past and on the future, the unknown and the abandoned, what had been lost and what had been squandered, on consolations and the promises of the future, etc. All of it like that, fairly messy. An invitation I don't believe I wasted. I went on my way, then, head bowed. I have no idea why, but whenever I think about time, I look down at the ground; maybe it's the only way I can distract myself, because I immediately set about scrutinizing the unforeseen details of its surface. I was headed for the end of the lake and kept noticing the imperfections in the dirt path that had stood up against people's footsteps.

In the past I used to think that the best way of spending my birthday was to keep hidden and opt for a one-day banishment: to leave home, go to the city's unknown or rarely visited district, and devote myself to roaming around for the day as if I were somebody else, or at least as if I didn't exist, or were indeed nobody; or to adopt some twenty-four-hour personality, etc. I'd take any train at all and get off at a remote station. Then I would set off walking, calmly and tirelessly, as if I'd arrived in another country once I stepped off the train. But I was in my own place, in my own city, I'd actually lived not far from there for a long time, a phase that now seemed to belong to somebody else, so that, alien to and simultaneously accustomed to that landscape, I kept recognizing the signs of my old life, although devalued. I was never capable of following other people, though the idea occurred to me more than once, as a subterfuge to while away these long, aimless birthday walks.

It could happen that not too far from the railway station, but far enough, I would come upon some solitary person walking through the empty streets—under such circumstances, tailing another person was impossible, because in those neighborhoods the itineraries are too short, and especially because I had no way of dissembling or fading into a landscape as barren and quiet as that, both of us, walker and pursuer, would be the only living creatures in the desert, and thus too visible, etc.—and so it could happen that if I saw someone in the empty streets, I'd feel an initial impulse to follow him at a discreet distance, but in the end I'd give up on it; the very desolation of the neighborhood would override any argument and conviction. It was as if the desire for adventure, for fiction to a certain extent, as I explained just now, which had originated someplace as a variant of curiosity, had dissolved before assuming any true form.

The atmosphere on the outskirts of the city turned out to be both intimate and alien to me; I could recognize the language, since I shared it, but I'd lost a bit—or a great deal, I don't know—of the pulse of its expressions and of the local idiom in general, its resonances. And so these birthday walks were approximate in more than one sense. My birthdays consisted of vague gestures of this type, an exile for a few hours toward a part of the past and toward a geographic area that no longer belonged to me, but because they'd been mine once, I had considered them united until that moment:

both parts were one and the same, a mixture of time and place. When the day was nearly over, I'd return from the outskirts as if I were coming back not from another reality, but rather, from a brother planet, an outlandish dimension into which I could set foot only once a year, when the calendar, underscoring my presence, so to speak, in the world, invited me by this same operation to suspend that presence, to doubt it, or at least, to hide it.

The path that ran along near the water kept displaying its neglected surface; in reality, I didn't expect it to change, but between one thought and another, some sideways glance at a distraction or some specific point in the landscape that called for my examination, I gradually arrived at the aforementioned place, the oblong building that stood at the lakeshore, with large, empty terraces on either side and great, wide windows that gave onto the water. One didn't need to examine it for long to know that it had been the old boathouse, converted at some point into a café, according to what it said on several lecterns on both terraces and on a sign over the entrance: CAFÉ DO LAGO. The structure was modest and embellished at once. As one could easily imagine, it was in the same style as the terrace on the plaza by the *pedalinhos*, as well as the guardhouses, or tool sheds, whatever they were, that were scattered across the park.

I went to sit down on the left-hand terrace, as far as possible from the water, from where I had a rather privileged view of the lake; I could also see, from the vertex of the old boathouse, how the panorama slowly opened out until it achieved its full breadth even beyond the swans' area, which now could be seen, on the left-hand shore, as a slightly undefined concentration, a mixture of trees and various facilities. While I was waiting to be served, I began to consider the most recent events. Obviously, the episode with the fish and the turtles, and the associated thought, too, which arrived like an instantaneous revelation, though I should have foreseen it: I was ensconced in my birthday month, and what's more, the day itself was only a few days off. By now I'm sufficiently acquainted with the fatal succession of nights—Borges said this, I believe—to understand that no distraction or idea can stop time from being realized and the future from arriving. It's not that I wanted to postpone my birthday, it was my certainty that it made no difference to start thinking about it in advance, though I hadn't expected to, in that park in the south of Brazil.

Then I happened to have the thought, as I mentioned before, of the two friends whose birthdays seemed to them an opportunity, or alibi, for writing about themselves in relation to time, or to life and its possible changes, and the impact all this had on them. And as I remembered them, an odd thing happened, my birthday vanished from the horizon as a looming eventuality, to assume the validity of the present itself. I felt, as I say, truly ensconced in the day of my birthday. I mean, in one way or another, reality had organized itself in such a way as to anticipate this date, and it inspired in me a feeling of solidarity and concord toward both friends and their books, and one of gratitude toward the carp and the turtles for prompting the moment and having allowed me to preside over that near-secret aquatic celebration. Consequently, from where I sat, I could devote myself to contemplating the calm waters of the lake, and also to reconsidering for a moment these most recent events and thanks to them, understanding that the whole park in its entirety had worked as an unexpected catalyst for my birthday.

A young waiter had left me the menu, only to take refuge immediately inside the café, probably wanting to benefit from the air conditioning. By now a brief age had gone by since his first appearance—short if one takes into consideration the span of a lifetime, long compared with the time most anyone would spend deciding what to order. For a moment, I thought I saw him keeping an eye on me from one of the windows. Not openly, like someone looking straight out, but diagonally, most of his body hidden behind the wall and his face peeking out a bit. I didn't give much thought to him, because at the same time I discovered I was being observed from another angle: swan No. 15 was headed right toward where I was sitting.

It had its eyes riveted on me, as if it were trying to memorize what it would say when it arrived and wanted to get a head start. I recognized the swan because the father and daughter were aboard, their heads peeking out from behind the animal's neck, one on either side. I recall that the girl was laughing as the father talked, and that her laughter became heartier just after her father said something and she looked at me. They were talking about and laughing at me, I supposed. It was the worst that could happen to me that day, being sensitized to the opinions of others in such a way. Perhaps I was mistaken, but it's not easy to overlook certain signs, especially when someone wants to disguise them. The swan kept coming nearer, despite almost touching the shore and having the entire lake to itself, spread out behind it like a mirrored metal fan, tinged slightly with green because of the reflections of the plant life. The father and daughter seemed to be in control of the boat; but seeing them like that, sunken up to their necks inside the enormous body, made me think of them as involuntary yet unnecessary participants in the actual scene that was unfolding.

The scene was the most bucolic of paintings or photos: the afternoon light, the lacustrine landscape, and eloquent in the foreground, the swan looking directly up the line of sight. It was looking at me, as I said, and would keep doing so even if I changed tables or left the terrace. It would keep on looking at me if I stationed myself to one side of the lake, even if I spied on it from behind a tree, or if I actually placed myself behind it. Even to me, one of the protagonists of the critical moment, what was happening was impossible. I started thinking about causes. It obviously involved a dramatic exaggeration. It's common to find eyes that look at us from paintings or photographs, as if they looked out once and for all, since they'll never look away from us while we are looking at them. One of the friends I've been mentioning has to this day never forgotten an event from his childhood when an older lady lavished praise on a painting whose model gazed at all times at whoever was beholding her.

For me, to compose a picture with that scene of the swan was at that moment the most immediate way of discovering a meaning in it, and that no doubt came about because of my feeling designated, chosen, somehow lionized by chance or fate on being the birthday boy. It was even possible that what I'd picked up on somewhat apprehensively—the father's derisive remarks to his daughter and her brief look—had in fact been a simple commentary, a piece of information, he told his daughter it was my birthday or that it was about to be, either way it was all the same, except that it would have been more inspiring if he'd said the latter, so that she had smiled shyly in my direction without knowing whether she should believe her father or not.

And I now recall Kentridge, the famous South African whose animated characters, especially one, named Felix—for whom he has a special affection, so much so that he seems to be an alter ego—rarely look out at the viewer. Nonetheless, they compensate for that characteristic, if indeed it must be compensated for and not entirely abandoned, by projecting visible gazes, I don't know of any better name for them. A visible gaze would be the path traced by someone's gaze, as if it were a beam of light or a luminous fluid. William Kentridge draws visible gazes by means of dotted lines, like those of the jets of water spurting in manifold directions in the fountain of the park I was in, which I described above. In this way, something physically impossible for painting or drawing to depict, as is the visual behavior of characters whose eyes we don't see, is successfully achieved. We can observe Felix with his back to us, or from the side, while he contemplates a point in the landscape, a corner of the room, or the stars in the firmament, and we note how intermittent dashes leave his eyes to make up the dotted line, giving the impression of a column of ants or an action in progress, in this case almost the same thing.

The gaze thus drops its habitual burden of passivity. The physical argument, possibly erroneous, that supports this idea, I suppose, is that light is not unduly speedy, and as a result contemplation itself can become material, and hence easily seen. The dotted lines represent not only a connecting link, but the gaze in a process of continuous renewal, stretched toward the point under observation, as if each line, no matter how small, were a concise or great concentration of energy shot from the eye which will, on reaching its goal, vanish. Kentridge is famous for his animated films in graphite that tell stories for adults in the style of the pioneers of animation. Sometimes he seems to seek to represent the insatiable appetite of the capitalist system, devourer of souls, bodies, and nature; at other times he presents graphic reflections charged with melancholy about feelings and human actions. By and large, I've been moved after witnessing the physical metamorphoses of his characters, who are subject to earthly forces that literally dissolve them, extinguish them, or reconfigure them in another form in the next drawing.

Once the scene in which they are the protagonists is over, these people yield to their own bodily transformation. One sees the silhouettes in motion and beholds the supreme weariness that overtakes these characters by the time they've nearly given their all; a moment comes when they appear to stumble, they get muddled in the forest of dashes the screen has become, and one frame later they've been dissolved or transformed. Needless to say, I feel more and more often like a Kentridge character, especially Felix, that errant being, someone versatile set adrift in history and the course of the economy, but at the same time exaggeratedly indolent in the face of what surrounds him, things or individuals, to the point where he succumbs with no sense of shock to the consequences, at times definitive, of his actions.

On the terrace of the Café do Lago, I was taking this in as the afternoon shadows lengthened: my day's walk, or perhaps my fast-approaching birthday as well, had united me still more with any of this artist's characters, especially during an episode's final vicissitudes, when they seem to get squashed, to dissolve among the elements or to vanish down the bathtub drain. I had the sensation of having been dragged to my table on the terrace, impelled by a private devotion, not overly fervent, but indeed pretty inertial, one that dwells on the minutiae of life and reality as a passport to daily existence. I imagined that as Felix I could fling myself into the lake and sink into its waters to drink them, through dozens of self-generated transfusion tubes; the next moment, the lake would empty, sublimating its waters toward the light of the stars and of something like the sun and the moon, a surrogate for the two, and I would remain in the middle of the empty pool, probably naked among the disabled swans, toppled and atilt on the earthen lakebed. The celestial body, moon or whatever it was, would shine, nearly full, and its alabaster reflection bathing the trees would be drawing's self-evident homage to the gray scale of photography . . .

The waiter had gone completely into hiding behind the window, and I began thinking of the strange coincidence of both my friends' beginning their birthday books with a reference to the moon. One presents his theory on the visibility of the moon, the other starts his story by practically commending himself to the lunar cycle, since he's setting out on a twenty-eight-day journey. I've known both men for years, and that's why I can say, based on experience, that we are, I with each of them, obedient to differing regimes of friendship. In the end, you could say the same of any relationship or person, and even more when you've reached a certain age, there are as many types of friendship as friends, though in my case it's worth clarifying, because there are some friends I've stopped seeing from one day to the next, with neither preambles or explanations. To describe what happened in detail would take me another book, probably of a more confessional tone, because I'd have to expand on my responsibility in the matter, or my share of responsibility, and I'd also have to explain the singular perception of time that, owing to those decisions, has been with me ever since. Is this related to my eternal sense of not getting any older, of feeling that the progress of time responds more to the peculiar elasticity of life's episodes than to an accumulation of events and years? I don't know. I could say I coexist with several hypotheses and that not one of them manages entirely to persuade me, when here comes a new criterion or substitute argument, the new idea that takes charge. The more I think, the less convinced I am; but it's not just a question of thinking: I'm actually proceeding in the realm of pre-cerebral intuitions. When I'm on the verge of sighting a definite theory, or a clear one at least, all at once the idea retreats, as if it were afraid of taking on an unexpected responsibility. And so the moon is an astronomical enigma for one, and a narrative clock for the other. I'm not about to discuss their points of view or their choices; I couldn't begin to do so even if I meant to. If I had to summarize, arbitrarily and in a few words, the sense I gather from both books, I would say that these two writers, on the eve of their fiftieth birthday, were attempting to show the system of beliefs that sustains them.

When I raised my eyes from my observation point on the terrace of the Café do Lago, I could make out some palm trees scattered as if at random throughout the park. Of course, only a few were actually visible, in fact no more than two or three, which stood like solitary columns above the rest of the trees and all the other plant life. During my walk I'd found it amusing to observe, time and again, the isolated plume of some one of them, as if it were definitively safe from any upheaval that might take place on the surface. I kept imagining that if the palm trees could think, and if they had time to harbor human feelings, disdain for the ground— for them no doubt a kind of despised and incomprehensible nether-world—would occupy a good part of their meditations. At the least sign of upheaval or turmoil, or indeed at any hint of activity on the lower level, that disdain would return each time, like a leitmotif, a recurrence that, far from making these trees suspicious of their own judgment and preconceptions, would confirm the appropriate-ness of their forebodings as well as the permanent chaos, as they saw it, from which they considered themselves safe. That reiterated thought, on the one hand, kept them safe, according to their logic, and was, at the same time, a concrete expression of their detach-ment from the ground.

I became completely self-absorbed during my walk and I told myself I'd never seen flora more autistic than these extremely tall palm trees, a probable consequence of their radical excess. Their autism appeared to be a sign of or condition for happiness, and as I walked about here and there and interrupted my thoughts to look up and see them standing erect like that in the most unexpected places, I felt a powerful sensation of envy, which led me to register with them a mental protest at the injustice of the situation: they were happy, indifferent to all that was earthly; and I was tormented by my doubts and worries, or quite simply condemned to scarcely take my eyes off the ground.

Very seldom had plants, generally speaking, induced feelings of empathy in me beyond the friendship you might feel as you pour water into your favorite flowerpot, for instance, or when you believe a modest spritz or some care will help the sick geranium. I also remembered the science experiments in school, especially the white beans or similar legumes set out to germinate, for which I used a glass jar and blotting paper soaked in water. And I told myself, on reliving it all, that my first and practically only experience of compenetration with the plant world dated back to that time; I don't know what to call it, a state of intense identification, perhaps even mystical, though always wrapped in domestic ceremonies, like watering or the eventual pruning, and tangible effects, like the changing of leaves, growth or attenuation. Every result of that past activity had obviously disappeared, for who knows where the old sprout can possibly be today, or the leaves fallen years ago. My habitual indifference to plants thus gave my unforeseen solidarity with the palm trees an added coloration, much more specific because of its contrast to my former disregard, even if from all standpoints unverifiable since I clearly couldn't take credit for the existence of those tall, healthy palm trees, of a perfect verticality and an enviable self-sufficiency, that was obvious.

In one open space in the park, astonishingly devoid of meaning because it was devoted to nothing in particular, I'd been able to come up to an exceedingly tall palm tree, maybe the oldest or the healthiest, at the base of which you got dizzy if you looked up. The ground in that spot was completely flat, and the tree thus formed a perfect perpendicular if you disregarded the logical thickening of the trunk before its base and above the ground. Consequently, the right angle could be verified from a distance, and up close would be refuted. I looked at the smooth trunk, to all appearances endless, so that it was hard to determine at which point it resolved into the fronds of the crown, which were long and curved downward under their own weight; I saw the trunk rising to that incredible point, at a distance that was possibly infinite, and told myself that perhaps the fronds were an expression of fear, or in any event, an improvised solution, because the tree itself considered it impossible to go on rising. Impossible, and perhaps useless too. At that moment, as I looked upward, overcome by vertigo, an idea occurred to me that even I found crazy: I longed to imagine the point from which a camera could take a picture of me at the foot of that tree, including the full height of the trunk beside me. I told myself it was probably impractical, since the camera would have to penetrate the deep underwood of the park and obstacles would intervene. If that image were possible, I'd look like a diminutive being, at the mercy of the whims of an outsized giant. What type of document would that photo be, I wondered. A moment from the naturalistic expedition, where the contrast with the majestic is a frequent and even obligatory step. I realized, then, that taking that photo was impossible, and still more, was inconceivable as fantasy, because the image created in my head proved more appropriate to tropical savannas, where the void finds its corroborating argument in those isolated, prominent trees. And in all likelihood that palm tree was nothing but that argument, the clearing's justification, that is, an allusion to much of the territory.

I remembered all this sitting at my table on the terrace, as the reflection on the lake gradually darkened. I've been a casual viewer of Kentridge's animated films. When I tried to get hold of one to watch at my leisure, it proved impossible. One time I managed to find a CD-ROM, but it was very costly and seems a joke, because it's got barely forty to fifty seconds of just a few of his works. Since it was old, I needed programs that no longer exist in order to run it. When I inserted it my computer began making a brand-new noise, like a vacuum cleaner's, that could be heard all over the house. Only after a great deal of effort and patience was I finally able to watch the disc, with the results just mentioned. In any case, though I consider myself a casual viewer of his work, and thus a mere admirer, I suspect that the recourse of the visible gaze was the initial find that allowed him to develop a good part of the rest.

I won't expand on this too much. My hypothesis is that at a subsequent moment the artist noticed that in the dramatic world of his drawings, it was unnecessary for objects or individuals to have eyes in order to establish mutual relationships. In the end, a dotted line was able to render a relationship that was as invisible as any gaze. This has made the drawings seem subject to a process of nonstop self-generation, it's something otherwise self-evident. It seems a world created out of geometry, and thus tending towards, or involuntarily, metaphysical. But this has also permitted a second success, I don't hesitate to call it that, which consists in highlighting the materiality of his work, its deep and genuine artifice, because the dotted lines exhibit the intensive construction that shapes them and organizes the work. It's a work that displays itself being made, insofar as the procedure—the lines and dots in constant transformation—is comprised in the sequential development of the stories. From the time of this discovery, my Felix of Kentridge (put that way, he sounds like a distinguished personage or a nobleman) became my secret coat of arms. I ought to say "my Felixes," since they take on differing personalities and are moved by different motives. For quite some time, in my private language—the unspoken one that belongs to me exclusively and which I use only in my constant mental soliloquies—to feel "like a Kentridge character" is my way of expressing the worst possible condition, the level beneath which one is unable to live. Feeling that way means being squashed to the ground, pulverized as a result of an act of vengeance of matter itself and undone until the next, but still uncertain, resurrection. Because apart from that, these characters have no moral alibi, they're not able to escape the blame or responsibility the story itself places on them. They can only express a diffuse suffering, between physical and spiritual, although they don't always do so, just like me. True suffering is a borrowed emotion, assigned by a viewer on seeing Felix's face in close-up as he looks at himself in the mirror, for instance, or when thanks to the transformation of his features, he reaches old age in two or sometimes three seconds.

I felt, then, that I was in the presence a painting of a lacustrine type. The swan was looking at me head on and fixedly, and the father and daughter, though only a few meters from where I sat, pretended to be absorbed in contemplating the environs. When the waiter emerged from the building to come to me, the swan began to retreat, surely thanks to the reverse capability of the pedal mechanism. It seemed to me to be backing off in order to make a final charge, but it promptly whirled around, pointing its tail to the right, and set off at once in forward gear. The *pedalinho* left the shore behind; I could now see the heads of the crew peeking out above the animal's hindquarters, probably unaware of what they were leaving behind them. A second later, the waiter arrived and I ordered a coffee.

An intense and perhaps prolonged digression then began, from which not even the waiter himself could distract me. The swan kept getting farther away, as if this were the end of a movie, or as if the father and daughter, reconciled with the animal world after their adventure, were truly able, thanks to the kindhearted bird that transported them, to find their way back home. I then imagined the lake and that same park as the anteroom of that great continent—the green denseness composed of plant life and mystery, devourer of people and dignities, pulverizer of souls, the implacable nature I referred to earlier, etc. I remained on the side of civilization, enacting one of the most habitual of writerly scenes: seated at a table in a café, the predictable backpack with literary tools inside it, a cup of coffee or some other vague drink in front of me; that is, circumstances favorable to writing.

I could take out my notebook and start controlling the navigation of my mind in a kind of semi-public session that everyone around me—though no one was present at that moment—would expect and tolerate. But I didn't do so, even after the waiter had already brought my order and nothing would interrupt me for a good while. The two writer friends have done it. I could even argue that those two books were written entirely in public places, almost exclusively cafés or similar locales. Why should I be any different? What circumstance keeps me from being just like them? I didn't find the answer then, and I don't have it now, either.

So on the one hand, I could find no reason not to set about writing in the Café do Lago, but on the other it's true that for some time

I'd begun to feel a sort of cautiousness, or insecurity, when, in one of the few cafés near my home, after certain preliminaries, I'd decide to open my notebook. I'd feel threatened, or closely observed. In fact, it was all in my head; no one was looking at me, or at anyone else. Until one afternoon, it must have been some two or three years ago, after focusing my mind on the idea of the threat—since I couldn't get over it—while the rest of the café's customers were reading or writing, carefree, a good number of them doubtless writers as well, I noticed that in fact something else was going on, though similar: what I felt was shame. I was ashamed to write, a feeling that still persists. And like everything shameful, if one wants to put it into practice, one has no choice but to do it surreptitiously.

For a long time I considered writing a private task, which at a certain moment nonetheless had to become public, because otherwise it would be very hard for it to stay alive, in particular and in general. My shame, though, proceeded not only from being engaged in something private in full view of everyone, but also from doing something unproductive, a thing both moderately useless and fairly banal. I felt they'd speak of me as a frivolous character, capable of squandering his time without concern, at a remove from any significant interest. And since I knew myself all too well, I had no choice but to concur with them in advance. Accordingly, my main worry wasn't so much overcoming my faults and my foolish illusions about writing, but rather, not being discovered. That's what life boiled down to, I could say as I approached a crucial birthday: not being discovered. All of us have one vital lie, without which routine daily existence would collapse; mine consisted of simulacra, in this case of literature.

Having so often adopted a writerly attitude, I ended up being a writer; and now, in a kind of retrospective panic, I was terrified they'd find me out, just when I was able to consider almost all the dangers cleared away. And the fear was reflected in what was most basic, as always: hands at work, the anonymous circumstance. I no longer feared not being published, or living far from success or recognition, I already knew that those things would always be within my grasp, for better or for worse; I feared that somebody, passing alongside my open notebook, would unmask me as a simple, deliberate impostor. The leaves of my notebook wouldn't contain sentences, or even words, just drawings that sought to simulate handwriting, or repeating pages with the word "what," especially "how," or with disconnected syllables that never made sense.

So I kept the backpack shut, didn't take out the book, much less the notebook, and once again passed up a session of writing that might have been fruitful, that sometimes happens, in order to sink into a diffuse meditation on the matters I'm in the process of recounting. The table was bare, except for the solitary cup of coffee. In the distance No. 15 looked like a white dot in slow flight, safe from any danger. I thought of my birthday, its charged imminence. Had my hour of reckoning arrived? With different emphases and arguments, one friend as well as the other counsel against it and refuse to take it on, though in their own way they engage in it, that I remembered pretty well. Accordingly, I thought it best to obey them.

Before my fear of being unmasked, to give it some name, café tables were promising places for me, spaces for materialization, where what was potential—poetic inspiration, literary expressiveness, whatever it may have been—used to become real. I had my protocols, like all writers, in any event not overly ambitious or complicated, after which I'd take out the notebook, read over what was most recent or maybe also what was least fresh, and after a few moments of taking stock, I'd dive into writing, without undue haste, but without distractions, either. Now my memory of those scenes is one of absolute happiness.

I wondered about the origin of that sensuality, ever-unsatisfied and ever-renewed, that led me to continue, unmindful of the interruptions, especially since writing in other places, non-public ones, say, subjected me to different experiences and feelings. I'm not talking about results, that would deserve other, less clear-cut explanations and conclusions; I mean the question of my location. The answer is grounded in my being a public writer, in a literal sense: writing in public, like a pianist who plays before an audience or a declaimer in the moment of acting. The incidentals didn't bother me, whether or not people were looking, nor if someone was secretly peeking into my notebook. There was something of a vocational commitment in that, a kind of anxiety that was unfocused and super-concentrated at once, until, after a brief moment of compenetration between my ideas' development and the colonized page, I would feel a slight tremor surrounding me.

Not my own tremor, the one that comes from true creation—which in any case I've never known—and leads one to hesitate, stumble, and at times even fall, so they say; but instead the tremor of the atmosphere surrounding me at that moment, which seemed intent on heightening the pressure in anticipation of an imminent blast, like those general quiverings which one finds difficult to ascribe to a visible source and which precede explosions or disasters in general. Yet I don't remember those moments as ones of mounting tension, or of menace, but, rather, of harmonious waiting. The atmosphere would begin to vibrate because something was happening, though nothing sufficiently important to call the attention of those present. The vibration concerned only me and was expressed, more than in an easily recognized change or rupture, in a sort of repressed contention of things: tables, display cases, chairs, counters, everything that made up the café. Objects lost their consistency or density, though not their form, and in a second reaction, since they couldn't explode, they became soft, springy, as if they were rubber or silicon models. Hence the reaction to the slightest current of air or of sound, expressed in a subtle, though massive, tremor that overcame the immobility of the ensemble, only to confirm it.

My two friends don't provide any significant details about their writing moments. They'd have no reason to. In any event, both mention them, and perhaps because of an excess of loyalty, or of feelings of indebtedness toward them, I now believe I should elaborate. I was saying, then, that things would go soft and begin to tremble. These were minimal vibrations, like electric ones or maybe sonic, who knows, which reminded me a little of the particular quivering of flan, when it shakes bashfully at a touch, as if it were afraid. That was the indication that something was happening in the session; compenetration, as I said, the absence of the surroundings, but its opposite, too, because it pertained to a private scale, my own scale of equilibrium or coexistence with the "publicness" I sought to attain. That is to say, what surrounded me was turning into a copy, it was a soft reality or soft version capable of including me. An anonymous scribe in a café governed by the murmurs of the congregation and the irritating sounds of the cups and dishes clattering behind the counter. Sometimes, if the things didn't go soft they could change color; barely a tinge, the next shade on the gray scale, which upset everything uniformly . . .

Contrary to the past, I was now sure that if I started writing in the Café do Lago nothing would tremble or change around me. Maybe that was the proof or the warning that I was going to be discovered and unmasked, I mean, that reality was no longer in solidarity with my activity, no matter what my compenetration; anyhow, I don't know, but what's certain is it ended up being my reason to feel a certain nostalgia for that past without cares or, more precisely, without fears. People were entering the terrace of the café and stopping to look at the lake, at the stand of leafy trees clustered to one side, they were even looking insistently toward where I sat, probably intrigued by this solitary and fairly unknown man. My dream, to be a nobody, a secret writer again, once more attained . . .

On the lateral path that led to the café, and that went on behind it to one of the park's exits, people would pass by every now and then, strolling along. At one moment it seemed to me that one of those people was the old man from the fountain, though at that moment I wasn't able to confirm it, a doubt that stays with me to this day. He walked without lifting his feet much, and so seemed to be dragging them, which I interpreted as a new sign of his definitive tiredness. For a moment I had a contradictory thought, that perhaps he was walking barefoot, because of a forgetfulness on waking hadn't put on the shoes he'd left to one side under the bench. I thought of going to retrieve them and then pursuing him to give them back.

Nevertheless, without deciding on doing anything, I sat contemplating the lake, which at that hour, nearly dusk, displayed a stillness that verged on the inert. I realized I could adopt for good the habit of visiting the Café do Lago to see the waters; or that I could run to inspect the bench beside the fountain, and in the event I found that gentleman's footwear, pursue him until I'd returned it. From that point on another story would develop, first of all a half-mysterious dialogue plagued by confusions, half-words and suspicions. The old man would tell me the story of his life without my having inquired, mixing political opinions and bitter commentary on his children or his niece and nephews.

And in this man's intention, more than in anything else, I would see myself reflected, better yet, I would feel myself interpreted. I said before, describing our encounter by the fountain, that he resembled me, or conversely, I resembled him; that we could even be the same person at different points in time. A specter from the future, an eloquent warning, but of unclear significance, aside from his zeal for walking.

What I want to say now is, as almost always, crisscrossed with imprecision. There on the terrace of the Café do Lago I ruled several things out, but I found myself in a kind of disjunctive: stay seated or run after the old man. It didn't occur to me to think that the following day I'd be going back to my country, dozing on the trip like the rest of the passengers. Immobility, waiting, and all related situations, on the one hand, and actions and exchanges with one's neighbor, on the other. I was searching for the delicate boundary between the two parts, as if I lived under protest in each of the two worlds. Needless to say, as has happened to me on other occasions, I arrived at no lasting conclusion, much less a self-evident one. As a disjunctive it was undoubtedly middling, but it seemed to be the only one to which I could aspire.

In general, I know that when speaking of private and opposing worlds, one tends to refer to divided, sometimes even irreconcilable facets of personality or of the spirit, each with its corresponding secret value and its psychological, metaphysical, political or simply practical—or even pathological—content. But in my case there was neither a moral nor existential disjunctive, what was more, I saw that my two worlds weren't separated in an equal or reciprocal way; neither did one world linger in the shadows or in private as the flip side of the other, the visible one, who knows which; nor would they seek to impose themselves over the other or to merge as one, by force or not, as tends to occur in these cases. Nothing of the sort; they seemed a nearly abnormal example of coexistence, of adaptive tendency and of absolute absence of contrasts. I took all this into consideration, and it seemed worrisome and insoluble . . . But an instant later I resigned myself, thinking that when all was said and done I ought to bow to these conditions, because just as we cannot choose our moment to be born, we also know nothing of the variable worlds we'll inhabit.

Sergio Chejfec, originally from Argentina, has published numerous works of fiction, poetry, and essays. Among his grants and prizes, he has received fellowships from the Civitella Ranieri Foundation in 2007 and the John Simon Guggenheim Foundation in 2000. His books have been translated into French, German, and Portuguese. He teaches in the Creative Writing in Spanish Program at NYU, and *My Two Worlds* is his first novel to be translated into English.

Margaret B. Carson translates contemporary poetry, fiction, and drama from Latin America. Her recent translations include Virgilio Piñera's "Electra Garrigó" and Griselda Gambaro's "The Camp," published in *Stages of Conflict: A Critical Anthology of Latin American Theater and Performance*. She teaches in the Modern Languages Department at Borough of Manhattan Community College.

Open Letter—the University of Rochester's nonprofit, literary translation press—is one of only a handful of publishing houses dedicated to increasing access to world literature for English readers. Publishing ten titles in translation each year, Open Letter searches for works that are extraordinary and influential, works that we hope will become the classics of tomorrow.

Making world literature available in English is crucial to opening our cultural borders, and its availability plays a vital role in maintaining a healthy and vibrant book culture. Open Letter strives to cultivate an audience for these works by helping readers discover imaginative, stunning works of fiction and by creating a constellation of international writing that is engaging, stimulating, and enduring.

Current and forthcoming titles from Open Letter include works from Catalonia, China, Czech Republic, Poland, Russia, and numerous other countries.

www.openletterbooks.org